My Private Calls

Jody Maxwell

While the callers in this book are real, all their names and most locations have been changed to protect their privacy. All names of public figures described in fantasies are strictly used fictitiously in imaginary actions and events, and are in no way to be taken as actually occurring or being real, unless specifically stated otherwise by the author. Names and locations described in sections about author's life are real, unless stated otherwise by author.

Copyright © 2004 by Jody Maxwell

All Rights Reserved, including the right to reproduce or transmit this book, or portions of it, in any form whatsoever without permission in writing from the publisher.

STEALTHCAT

PUBLISHING

Stealthcat Publishing

P.O. Box 26185

Overland Park, Kansas 66225-6185 USA

ISBN: 1-59457-661-0

To order additional copies of books or audio books please visit our website at www.jodymaxwell.com.

Printed in the United States of America

Cover Design and Artwork by Les Barany and Toby Dammit

For that person who had faith in me and was with me all the way, and to my family and friends whom I love and cherish

ACKNOWLEDGEMENTS

I want to especially thank Bruce who patiently accepted the disruptions caused by the thousands of calls over the years, and assisted as the technical computer guru in putting this book together.

I also wish to particularly thank Jim S., who always believed in me, and supported, coached, advised, and helped me, and without whom this book would not have been written; my lifelong friends for always being there and giving me encouragement, Mary Luttrell, Deanna Rudd, and Jim Shugart; Samantha Fox and Annie Sprinkle, for their constant friendship and support; my friend and confidante, Debi Ward, who frequently made the calls a little easier; Bill Wilson and his staff at Personal Services Club for all their work, so I could simply do the calls, wherever and whenever I wanted; Colleen, Tami, and Rhonda for the friendships we formed while they were doing terrific work giving me input on the callers.

An enormous thanks goes to a special Hungarian, Les Barany, for his help with the book by providing his wonderfully creative, artistic guidance.

I also offer Kudos to Toby Dammit for his great work on the cover of the book.

Many thanks to John Rieck for all his gracious assistance on the publishing of this book.

Thank you to Robert Guinsler, who gave me positive suggestions regarding the book's contents, and to Sterling Lord, for putting Robert and me in contact with each other.

There are so many really good people I was fortunate enough to get to know because of my career that I could not begin to name all of them, but I would like to recognize just a few of my favorites: Juliet Anderson, R. Bolla, Lisa Brenkman, David Christopher, Zebedy Colt, Gerard Damiano, Erica Eaton, Larry Flynt, Jamie Gillis, Diane Hansen, Veronica Hart, Lisa Hoffman, Ron Jeremy, Gloria Leonard, Radley Metzger, Michael Morrison, Manny Neuhaus, Michael Poulos, Katherine Reid, Patricia Reshen, Rita Ricardo, Vince Stanich, Ron Sullivan, and Jake Teague.

I owe a definite thank you to Al Goldstein, who early in my career became a true, lasting friend, and always stood by me.

There are certain people for whom I feel a tremendous gratitude for their lifetime loyalty and special friendship, including Mike Brittingham, Jay Cooper, Nancy Eicholz, Charlie Erickson, Chris Gatzoulas, Pat Gordon, Sandy Martin, Jim Mayer, Jim and

Helen McMullin, John Parr, Richard Patterson, Dian Robinson, Judy Sansale, and Dickie Bird Saunders.

My life has been enriched by knowing many exceptional people. These are just a few of them to whom I say thank you: Bobby Bell, Ron Berry, Tim Boxer, David Braude, Skip Burton, Mary Lou Cahill, Mark Carvel, Barry Chusid, Mike Compton, Richard Creighton, Bruce David, Joao Fernandes, Barbara Fried, Carol Gavin, Stan Glazer, Carol Gordan, Richard Keith, Lou Kirchner, Tom Leathers, Mike Livingston, Barbara Maggio, Denny Matthews, Edie McClurg, Jim M., Joe Meyers, David Moak, Roger Moore, Frank Morgan, Johnny Ray, Paul Sherman, Bill Shugart, Michael Solomon, Jan Stenerud, Oliver Stone, Lee Thornburg, Cathy Toohey, Mark Wells, Ralph and Jan White, Wade Williams, and William Wolf.

During my previous, longtime involvement within the Republican Party, which made up so much of my life, I have known many remarkable people. I wish to acknowledge just a few of them, including Richard Berkley, Christopher "Kit" Bond, George Gray, Ray James, Dennis McDonald, Bill Phelps, and John Sharp.

I would be remiss if I didn't express my appreciation for a few of my newer friends, who came into my life and added so much to it by their friendship: Andrew B., Pam B., Russell Cox, Janeen Davidson, Vivian H., John and Holly Knox, Tim and Peggy Morris, Doris Ow, Jerri and Ken Tehee, and Wendy W.

I also wish to thank Hearne Christopher, Jr., for his

encouragement and his terrific help in tracking down some factual information for the book.

There are so many people to whom I owe thanks, my other personal friends with whom I have shared, and spent, so much of my amazing life, some of whom are mentioned in this book – you know who you are.

I must not forget all the callers with whom I talked during my 12 years having fantasy calls. Without them there would not have been this book, or my future books, sharing my private calls.

Contents

Introduction	xvii
In The Beginning	1
The Break-in Call	2
First Time	4
Chapter 1	
Toys	**7**
Louie's Toy	9
The Swing	10
Harold's Toys	14
Horny Midwest Attorney	17
El Paso Rudeness	19
Chapter 2	
The Fans	**25**
Summer Phone Fling	28
New York Groupie	29
Dallas Fan Club	32

Panties For Sale	37
Minneapolis Moments	39
Erotic Film Dancer	46
Presidential Chat	49
Prescription for Pleasure	
Attorney Career Change	54
Just Chit-Chat	59
Vancouver Small Talk	60
Jody's Therapeutic Call	62
Not for Sale	64

Chapter 3
Swinging Days   67

Ultimate Caribbean Cruise	69
Calgary Threesome	72
Afternoon Delight	79
Rich's Heat Trigger	81
Horny KC Fireman	84
Orgy in Ontario	88
Emmitt's Cruel Punishment	90
Stressed Air Controller	93
Swinging Fascination	98
Xmas After-Party	99
Wild Fantasies	101
Hollywood Threesome	106
Naughty Nicole	108
Minnesota Swingers	112

Chapter 4
Different Strokes   117

Sexy Aunt Mary   119
Smoke Rings   121
Bob's Screen Play   123
The Narcissist   126
The Power of Tits   129
The Cold Architect   130
Crotchless Panties   137
The Round Bed Hang-Up   139
The Milk Man   141
Soldier Boy   142
The Spandex Man   145
Peeping-Tom Fantasy   147
Water Sports   153
Cross-Dresser   156
Shoelace Fetish   159
Surgery Dilemma   162
Milwaukee Brewmaster   165
Nuclear Fantasy   167

Chapter 5
Trips To Paradise   175

Rockin' Canoe   177
Sailboat Seduction   178
Sex On The Beach   181
B & D Oil Executive   185
The Dirty Baker   187
The Mile High Club   189
California Beachhead   190

Lonesome in New York	196
Jamaica Jamboree	198
Dinner at the Falls	200
Cinema Delight	203
Stressful Trial Attorney	205
Fargo Body Builder	207
Memories from Rio	209

Chapter 6
Bon Appétit

Oral Fixation	216
"Greek" and "Head"	218
Lick Them Clean	220
Jody's Challenge	222
World Traveler	225
Ivan the Great	228
Winter Heat In Saskatoon	230
Pre-Meeting Ecstasy	232
The Graduate	234
On The Road Again	239
Snow Bound	2
Troubled Welder	243
Lonesome in Folsom	247
Oral Only, Please	249
The Shy Exhibitionist	250
Heated Waterbed	253
A Perfect Cut	261
Office Seduction	262
Executive Runner	264
New York Quickie	266
The Ultimate Dream Wake Up	268

Sean's Favorite Couch   272
Rocket Man   275
Lookin' for Love   277
Speedboat #69   279

Chapter 7
The Caboose   **283**

The Gentle Doctor   285
Let Me Talk Sexy   287
Jody's Sleeping Aid   289
A Real Ass Man   292
Back Door Fantasy   294
No Dirty Talk   296

After Thoughts   **299**

INTRODUCTION

I began thinking about writing a book on fantasy phone sex the day I signed the contract with Personal Services Club, considered the Rolls Royce of phone sex clubs and companies. However, it was not an idea I could turn into a decision so quickly. Initially, I thought if it worked out, and I enjoyed it, then, I should write a book, and share with others the mysteries of phone sex.

My life in erotica had begun about nine years earlier, when I had just graduated from the University of Missouri. A few months before graduation, Gerard

Damiano (of ***Deep Throat*** morality panel on campus. I met him afterward at the press conference, when I interviewed him. Damiano and I got along very well, and he invited me to come to New York after graduation for a screen test. After giving it careful thought I decided to do it.

Since that successful screen test, I had starred in erotic films and on stage. I had written monthly columns and feature stories, of all kinds, for popular, national adult men's magazines, such as ***Cheri Escapade***, among others, and had even been on the editorial staff of ***Cheri.*** My interviews, and stories about me, had appeared in hundreds of magazines and newspapers. I had been a guest on radio and television talk shows, coast-to-coast.

My life in erotica included meeting various famous and amazing people, and being exposed to many unusual experiences, by most standards, in the previous nine years. However, I was totally ignorant about the world of phone sex.

Then, during one of my starring engagements on stage, at O'Farrell Theater, in San Francisco, my friend, fellow erotic film star, Juliet Anderson, approached me about having phone calls with my fans. Juliet was already with Personal Services Club, and had been asked by the owner, Bill Wilson, to tell me about it, and to get my permission for him to call me.

Her enthusiasm enveloped me so much, that I decided to talk with Bill, to hear the nuts and bolts of this service, and what he had to offer to both his clientele and to me. The idea of talking one-on-one with my longtime fans was appealing. I liked the idea

I could actually chat with some of the people who had followed my career.

Before talking with Bill, I did my own checking, and discovered he had a very good reputation, and was well liked by his employees. This was important to me because if I had received a bunch of negatives, I would not have ever considered getting involved in phone sex. The business of erotica is tough enough without deliberately asking for problems.

Early on, I was impressed with Bill Wilson's operation. I visited with his management people, the screeners, and many of the house girls. The consensus was that Wilson treated all his employees and associates, such as the stars, fairly and decently. He also was extremely protective of everyone connected to his organization.

I observed another interesting fact. Personal Services Club only had female employees, no matter what the positions. Talking to the ladies, I discovered many of them had been with Bill for years. In these kinds of businesses, that in itself is worthy of the highest of accolades.

I decided to go with Personal Services Club and I signed a contract with them as an Independent Contractor. Wilson's exclusive list of stars was composed of all independent contractors. While the house girls got paid hourly wages and bonus percentages for over a certain number of minutes per call, the stars generally had a set time frame of fifteen minutes per call, with some exceptions. The stars worked out how much they wanted to charge with Bill Wilson. The percentages for the split were in the contracts. As a result, while most stars charged about the same, some occasionally chose some other amount. The stars' fees usually ran from fifty dollars to ninety dollars per fifteen minutes.

Like the rest of the stars, I could be "on" as often or as little as I pleased. Wilson sweetened the pot by giving the stars a little extra hourly money just for being available for calls. He also supplied each of us with a private phone line at our homes, exclusively for our calls, for which he paid the monthly expenses. None of the stars worked from his offices. We did our calls from home, on the road, anywhere we liked.

We did not have the problems of checking in after the calls to say whether the call was five minutes or fifteen minutes. When a member requested me or another star, he was told up front that he would be charged the full amount for the call regardless of how little or how much of those fifteen minutes he used. The screeners handled all the money, billing and business matters. All I, and the other stars, had to think about was the caller and his fantasy. If a caller cheated Personal Services out of their money for a call with anyone, star or house girl, she would still be paid. Wilson's theory was that any girl who did a call deserved to be paid for that call.

Personal Services did things differently from other phone sex services. Most used 900 numbers or something similar, and the callers would automatically be billed on their phone bills.

Wilson decided early on that would be a hassle.

Instead, at Personal Services, the caller was required to call and talk to a screener, and the caller would have to have his name and number listed in the phone book. If he had an unlisted number, than he would have to pre-pay, by sending a check or money order, until they felt comfortable with him as being legitimate and of legal age. Assuming the caller was listed, then, the star or house girl, would call the client back as a collect call. If the person was at his office, hotel, or somewhere else, where he did not want a collect call, he could receive a direct call for an additional fee.

There was a zero tolerance policy about certain kinds of calls at Personal Services Club. Absolutely no calls involving children in fantasy sex were allowed. No calls involving the girl or the star being hurt, hit, brutalized, or injured in any way, in the fantasy talk, was tolerated. Also, no scatological fantasies were permitted. Everybody connected with Personal Services loved this policy.

While the policy was logical and correct, it did not make any of us immune from receiving other highly unusual, odd, or bizarre calls occasionally. Some were on subjects totally opposite my personal tastes, to the point they were an absolute turn off. The times I received any such call, I would have to reach deep within myself and pull out my acting skills to successfully do the call. I have excluded the most extreme calls of this nature from this book. I have included some of the less extreme odd calls, to give the reader a chance to see inside the heads or minds of a few of these callers, and to be amused or amazed, or even befuddled, by what turns some people on. I never judged these callers. After all, their fantasies were harmless to other people. I simply found their fantasies to not be of any interest to me.

Personal Services Club had some "specialty" house girls, as do most fairly large phone sex services. One of the most popular house girls was a medical student at UCLA, who, at the time, was studying to be a psychiatrist. She was a very pretty, very sweet girl whose specialty was domination. Virtually, all the men who called her were submissives. She paid for her education by doing phone sex calls.

There were others, of course. Big-breasted women were always hugely popular. Boyishly-built girls received lots of calls. There was a girl who specialized in being a submissive, as long as it was kept within the boundaries of the house rules. Of course, most the girls did general calls, and did not have a specialty. The stars received calls from fans, first, and the general calls, second.

Some people wonder how callers find out about the various companies and clubs, which offer phone sex. Men's magazines, the Internet, television, ads on x-rated videos, and in adult product catalogs are the primary sources for advertising phone sex services. Since phone sex gives a sense of privacy and anonymity, which is wanted by the callers, word of mouth is not a viable means of promoting the services. That has never deterred phone sex from being a major player as a moneymaker.

The fact is there are many thousands of people

who practice fantasy phone sex every day, and not only men calling to speak to women. There are women clientele who talk to men. Gay services are popular. Couples call a phone sex service to safely add a little spice to their love lives. Fetish lovers can find their secret desires fulfilled by specialized phone sex services. That's only the paying clientele. An untold number of private people practice phone sex with their partners or lovers every day, without the involvement of money. As far as the professional side though, it is a multi-billion dollar industry, with the money spread throughout thousands of services worldwide.

A couple of the primary reasons fantasy phone sex does so well is because it is in that family of great equalizers, as long as a person can pay for it. It does not matter whether the caller is rich and famous, or humble and middle class. He can be a famous basketball player or a Ford Motor Company assembly worker. The caller can be a high office holder or a sanitation engineer. Looks or disabilities are irrelevant. Neither race nor age are factors for enjoying fantasy phone sex. Also, for many, it is the ultimate definition of safe sex.

Phone sex became a household word in the late 1990's when the President of the United States, Bill Clinton, made headlines regarding his alleged phone sex with former White House staffer, Monica Lewinsky. Since then, phone sex is an ongoing object of humor by many top comedians. It is frequently mentioned in movies, on popular sitcoms, and serious drama.

phone sex seems to have found its own lasting niche in the world of erotica.

Since I decided to write about phone sex from day one, I kept extensive records during my years in the business. However, to protect the privacy of my previous callers I have changed their names and most locations for this book. I tried to keep similarities between the original locations and the new ones. For example, a southerner will still be located in the South. Otherwise, I have attempted to portray all the calls in this book as accurately as possible, including the erotic, explicit, and slang terminology used by the callers during their calls.

Since I exactly described the calls, a great many of them will show that, frequently, callers desired a variety of fantasy sexual activities during their calls, not simply one basic act.

As a result, I found it a difficult task to group the calls after I finished writing all the ones for this book, because the majority of them could have gone in several different groupings. Quite frankly, it became mainly a matter of personal judgment determining where to place most of the calls. The preponderance of the calls in this book could have been placed in a variety of categories.

Also, I did not let the tidbits relating to my life and career, beginning, and woven through, each chapter, affect or influence my writing of these true stories.

I hope anyone reading this book will come away feeling more enlightened on a subject frequently mentioned, but of which not much is known by most people. With **My Private Calls**, I have tried to uncover some of the mysteries and attractions to a pastime practiced by many thousands of people everyday in this country alone, and many more thousands worldwide.

IN THE BEGINNING...

Although I have placed my calls in chapters, based on the fantasies of the callers, I decided to share my very first two calls as appetizers, preceding the chapters. Many "firsts" are memorable, and that's how I view my initial two calls. After all, many women, regardless whether or not they are stars, never make it beyond their first couple of calls because of what they consider their awful experiences. I was lucky because mine went fine.

In my case, while I did have a touch of stage fright ahead of time, I settled down when I was finally "on."

s went well, and they were the opening of a gig with a long, twelve-year run.

In the beginning, there was hot and sexy Troy, followed by sweet George. I was getting the hang of it by the end of the second call.

Enjoy my inauguration to fantasy phone sex, and prepare for an intriguing journey into the hearts and souls of callers' most intimate desires.

The Break-In Call

When I signed the contract agreeing to have phone calls with my fans and other callers, I wondered how tough it would be to talk extemporaneously with strangers, who more often than not wanted to feel sexually satisfied by the end of the call. I was expected to verbally fulfill their fantasies, which could run the gamut from the most ordinary, basic sex to more diverse kinds. The screeners, who talked to the clientele before the calls took place, told me some callers would find sexual pleasure in things that really did not have anything to do with sex. There would also be callers who just wanted to chat. As a result, I was pretty nervous when my first call came, not knowing what to expect.

My initial call came from Troy, who lived in Philadelphia. The screener told me that Troy requested to "break me in." This was his "thing," his fantasy. He had developed rapport with the screeners, who answered the phones, and took care of the business matters, before I, or anyone, received calls. As a result, he had a standing order for any star's first call. Of course, he talked to the girls other times, too, but the first calls were a big deal to him.

Troy was notified I was on for the very first time. I found him to have a sexy voice with a pleasant demeanor. He told me that he always got especially turned on having these "virgin" calls. He said if I had any problems he would help me through them, but that he was a basic kind of guy and he was already a fan of mine, having followed my career. He was something of a talker, so I didn't have to say too much during my opening call.

The sexy part of our conversation begins when Troy tells me he loves large breasts and likes to fuck them. Mostly, he describes the action. I interject a few comments occasionally. Then, he tells me he loves pussy eating, as he details what he is doing to me. He still insists on doing most of the talking. When he is good and hot, he wants me to suck him. At that point, he lets me talk. I take over the verbalization of the fantasy, and am totally successful at getting him off in this manner.

Afterward, Troy told me I was delightful, and completely successful with my first call. Of course, I knew he contributed a great deal to the favorable outcome of the conversation.

On the other hand, I wasn't too nervous any longer, thanks to him. Troy's attitude and talking had made it so much easier than it might have been. I was always grateful to Troy for making that first call so painless.

* * * *

First Time

My second caller was a very nice fellow, in his early thirties, named George, from Massachusetts. He was a little nervous when he called, but so was I since he was only my second call. I was already learning that I really did have to be able to think and respond quickly to the caller's requests. Also, figuring out how to use the fifteen-minute window most efficiently was going to definitely take practice.

George immediately told me that he had never called a phone sex club before. I put him at ease by telling him I was new to it, also. He, further, explained he was a virgin and that he had a slight case of cerebral palsy.

I liked George. He was sweet and shy. What he wanted was to hear a woman tell him about making love to him. He wanted to be fussed over and guided. George dreamed of having oral sex and intercourse with a woman who would ignore his condition. That was his "dream-wish."

For George's fantasy, I come into the room wearing red and black lingerie. I talk seductively to him, and I kiss him. I rub my body against his. Then, I perform fellatio on him, describing it in detail. Finally, I remove the lingerie and I have intercourse with him to his successful completion.

George was very happy at the end of the call. He thanked me for fulfilling his fantasy. So, I was not surprised that he became a regular caller.

CHAPTER 1

TOYS

Sexual toys have always been around going back to the earliest times. While I was in college, I studied ancient Greek theatre, in one of my courses, and I learned that in ancient Greece, several of the more delightful and long-lasting comedies were written. Some of these plays are still presented on stage today. In a number of them, references are made to sexual toys. For example, in one of the most popular and enduring ancient comedies, all the women in a certain town had access to what were the existing forms of dildos, at that time, for their use when their men were away at war.

The only thing that has changed since ancient times is that there are now greater varieties, better made, and more sophisticated toys, available for both women and men.

I had been aware of various sexual toys before I ever entered the world of erotica. I had even received some as a practical joke at a surprise birthday party given for me a couple of years before getting into the business. However, when I began making erotic films, my exposure to intimate adult toys greatly increased.

In my first erotic film, **Portrait,** several toys were used, including a regular, flesh-colored dildo, a cranking, twisting, moving dildo, and a very large double-headed dildo (a head on each end). These toys successfully and visually served their purposes in that movie.

Another of my movies, a pastoral, period piece, contained vegetables and fruits from the garden, which became the logical toys for this particular film. This was a good example that all adult toys do not have to be high tech, yet, still can be fun.

One of my movies, **Outlaw Ladies**, had another actress, in the film, using a somewhat different-looking, skinny dildo for the purpose of receiving anal pleasure.

Most adult movies use toys sometime during the movie. They are great visual aides and they add a little different touch and variety to the films.

Continued on page 12

Louie's Toy

My first week doing phone sex introduced me to all kinds of guys. One of them was Louie from Napa, California. While, at first, it seemed Louie was pretty standard in his interests, I quickly discovered he had his own sense of what was standard.

After briefly introducing himself, Louie told me he was into anal sex. Only Louie had a little different take on the subject. Before he had fantasy sex with me, he told me he actually had a large dildo up his ass, which he put there just before he called.

Louie begins his fantasy by wanting me to screw him in the ass with his dildo as a prelude to other sex. He also wants me to suck him, at the same time. Louie asks me to orally describe all this in minute detail, which I do, for the first half of his fantasy.

After that part of the call, Louie decides he wants to go down on me. At this point, Louie is doing the talking. He goes into specifics. Then, he requests to have intercourse with me, which he has me describe. For his grand finale, he

wants anal sex with me, which is how he finally gets off. At the end of the fantasy, Louie tells me he left the large dildo in his ass during all the phone sex.

As time progressed, I discovered Louie wasn't the only man, who fantasized about anal sex. Many callers did. I also found, after many more calls, that Louie wasn't the only caller who liked to use toys during the calls.

* * * *

The Swing

I first heard from John on a rainy, September morning. John worked for the Port Authority in New York, and lived in a converted flat in lower Manhattan. He said he had a steady girlfriend. However, after seeing my movie, **Neon Nights**, John wondered if I would "swing" with him, anyway.

I had been in this industry for many years and I thought I knew what he had in mind. I was wrong. Men's sexual fantasies vary, but his was -- shall I say unusual. I was blown away with such a creative, sexual intellect.

John explained to me what he and his girl friend would occasionally do.

He has a king-sized bed under a huge window in his fourth floor bedroom, located in a former old warehouse. Also, John has mirrors on the ceiling, and a large pulley, with the rope connected to an electric motor that is controlled at the headboard.

His girlfriend gets naked, and straps herself in a harness similar to the supports hospitals use to elevate broken legs. She sits on the bed, and secures thigh and calf supports to the device. Then, he pulls her up. Her legs are straight together, raised approximately 6 to 8 inches above her ass. He raises her about 5 feet from the ground. Then, he gets under her, and moves into the "ready" position. Next, he lowers her very slowly until he has penetrated her, (he never asks her if she is ready). He reaches over and spins her legs around while inside her. As the rope is twisting and cinching up from the spin, he hunches up with her as far as he can go, and, then, he spins her down the other way and back up again. He says he always cums on the second spin.

This was not a normal phone sex call. He did not get off (at least not on this call), but really enjoyed telling me how he and his girlfriend "swing," sometimes. He continued to describe all the different positions the two of them had tried, even changing places, which, he said, was a little more difficult because of her limited mobility. He was positioned downward, and had to control the spin, while she was high on her back and her hands were not free. He had different names for them, but the Maxwell Oral Spin (named after me) was one of his favorites.

John called many times following that first call and always wanted to know if I would spin with him. I always said, yes, please spin me!

Continued from page 8

Although I never made short hardcore films or loops, I did make a single, special, soft, short film on one occasion. When I was with *Cheri*
produced a small, sexy, hot little film, to sell to fans. There was nothing hardcore in this film, but there were lots of dildos, as I used them for demonstrations in it. My film could only be purchased through *Cheri* or me. Since I was essentially by myself, the dildos made great props.

To make this special film, a variety of dildos were needed. Since they can be bought in many places, I these toys.

However, I did insist on one thing. I needed to pick them out myself.

The senior editor of the magazine decided to find where I could pick and select from the largest variety.

After he researched the matter, he came to me one day, and said he had found the perfect place from which I could choose them.

Late the next morning, we grabbed a New York cab, which took my editor and me to an address in a warehouse district in Manhattan. I looked around but didn't see any stores. This is when Peter, my editor, told me he had found a dildo factory and had made arrangements for me to choose whatever I desired.

We entered the place, which was not open to the public. The sight that greeted us seemed surreal. It was a huge warehouse, completely filled, up to about twenty feet high, with rows upon rows, of dildos. They were all in clear plastic wraps in clear containers. Dildos were everywhere. As I walked down the aisles between rows I felt like I must have stepped into paradise for women. I had never dreamed, nor imagined, there were so many varieties, colors, sizes, and types of dildos in my life. I could hardly comprehend what I was seeing I was so amazed.

Picking out the right dildos should have been an easy no-brainer decision but, instead, became a major project. I had to look at, study, touch, think about what to get. I was totally overwhelmed by the fact – I asked how many – there were approximately one million dildos surrounding me!

I had such a tough time figuring out what I wanted for my own little film that we ended up spending approximately two hours in the warehouse, by the time I finally made my choices.

Continued on page 22

Harold's Toys

Every once in a while I would get a call, which I found so unusual, I was not really sure what to say. When the screener called to give me the information regarding this gentleman, she mentioned he was into humiliation and being extremely dominated. I had my qualms about doing this call, because these were not things in which I was particularly knowledgeable, as I was not into them myself. I really wasn't interested in extreme domination and humiliation. However, the screener told me this man had requested me, and she persuaded me to talk to him.

compared to any others I had ever had. He didn't waste a lot of time on small talk, but he did tell me he was thirty-seven years old, about 5 feet 11 inches tall, average build, brown hair and eyes. Harold said he was the general manager of a manufacturing company.

Then, Harold immediately told me he had all his paraphernalia next to him when he called. He said that included nylon cord, ball and cock harnesses, dildos, various weights, butt plugs, 7 Gates of Hell, and a ball spreader.

When Harold finished his laundry list of toys, I actually was speechless! I didn't have a clue what some of these things were. I had considered myself intellectually quite knowledgeable about items used for erotic play; yet, Harold had thrown me a curve. Besides, Harold said he actually had these items and he wanted me to order him to use them and to tell him how. He said he was going to do the things I said, in real life. I reminded him it was fantasy phone sex.

Harold told me exactly what he wanted me to tell him to do, at that point. He had it pretty much scripted. He also said he wanted to be called a "sod, a dumb, lifeless clump of dirt." Later, he requested I call him a "lifeless, lowly worm."

One of Harold's earliest requests, and he was specific, was he wanted me to order him to tie up his testicles and penis with the nylon cord. He also wanted me to tell him to anally use a dildo on himself. He named some of the various items and how he wanted to use them.

I spent a lot of time listening to Harold work himself up. I was glad about that because it meant less talking from me. He described all his unusual actions in great detail. He even added some kind of icy hot lotion to the mixture.

Harold wasn't satisfied with just the call though. He wanted instructions for after we were ***off***
telling him what to leave attached, for him to wear under his clothes to a topless club's restroom, and, then, to work the next day.

The call was certainly different from any I had ever had. I was still somewhat puzzled by some of Harold's toys, but Harold had made it clear he enjoyed the call. That being the case, I thought the call was completely finished when we hung up. I was wrong.

There was a footnote, of sorts, to this call. Harold surprised me by sending me a photo, by way of Personal Services, of himself, with all these gadgets and items attached to him. It was an amazing sight! I knew I wouldn't forget Harold anytime soon.

* * * *

Horny Midwest Attorney

One night I received a call from a screener telling me that one of my fans was waiting for me to call him at a Howard Johnson's in the Midwest. Actually, this was not unusual, as a certain percentage of callers did call from motels and hotels. The screener told me he was someone to whom I had spoken previously.

My fan, Carson, was anxiously waiting by the phone, when I returned his call. He was in a chatty mood on this occasion. He began talking to me about his trip, explaining why he was at a Howard Johnson's. In past calls, Carson hadn't told me much about his professional life, but this time he wished to speak about it.

Carson told me he was an attorney on the staff of a prominent state attorney general, in the Midwest. This was a business trip, he said, involving securities and fraud and an out-of-state company doing business in his state. He continued talking about the case a little longer. Then, he added a few comments about the attorney general's office before he was ready to leave this topic.

That night, Carson had been out to dinner and the lounges with some fellow attorneys, and they had been drinking champagne. He loved California champagnes, and California music, too, like The Beach Boys, he said. Carson was in a lively mood after all the bubbly. He was slowly chatting his way to his phone sex fantasy.

Finally, Carson was ready to actually talk about his desires. He wanted me dressed in a sexy, black, lacy teddy, and garter belt, stockings, and hi heels. Carson desired for it to take place in a motel in a regular double bed. He said he liked the closeness of being near a woman in a double bed.

Carson tells me he wants to watch me massage my breasts, and, then, pull down the top of my teddy and completely expose my breasts to him. He asks me to play with my breasts and slowly squeeze my nipples until they are extremely hard.

Now, he requests I masturbate in front of him. Carson gets naked, and sits on the side of the bed watching me as I sensuously handle my breasts. I lie down on the bed and remove my teddy. I play with myself, running my hands all over me. Carson's body responds as he strokes himself, while constantly observing me.

In his fantasy, he hands me a vibrator and expects me to use it, at this time. I take the vibrator and use it on myself. He desires for me to be very aroused, on the verge of climaxing. Suddenly, he cums both on my breasts and on my face.

Carson clearly enjoyed himself. He liked talking to me, and he was totally into his fantasy. Interestingly,

Carson's overall fantasy was essentially the same as in our previous conversations, with minor variations.

When we were about to hang up, Carson told me he felt so relaxed he was going to get a good night's sleep no matter where he was. He also mentioned he would be back for more in the near future.

* * * *

El Paso Rudeness

Sometimes, when a screener phoned with the information on a caller, the screener would warn me that the caller had developed "a reputation," with the service. Probably, the most common warning was that the caller was rude in some manner. Since rudeness was not a threatening or criminal act, those calls were usually accepted. While I had been warned many times, usually this was not a problem with my calls. That was one of the advantages of being an erotic film star. Most of the time, I, and the other film stars, were fortunately treated with more respect and deference than the house girls. However, there were exceptions. A call I received this particular night came with the "rude" warning.

The caller's name was Barry, who resided in El Paso, Texas. Barry, the foreman of a cattle ranch, described himself as 6 feet tall, weighing 230 pounds, with dark brown hair, brown mustache, and brown eyes. He claimed to have a really thick 8-inch cock, and he said he was a pussy and ass man.

So far, Barry had not shown any of the rudeness of which I had been warned, but he was anxious to get to his fantasy.

Barry's phone fantasy begins with us being in an apartment together in San Francisco. He wants soft music, wine, and candlelight in the bedroom. He immediately starts by going down on me, and fingering me, at the same time. He describes his technique in great detail. Next, Barry uses a vibrator in my pussy, and while continuing that, he inserts a second vibrator in me, anally. That's not everything that is happening in his fantasy. He also has me sucking him while the two vibrators continue their action. Barry requests I deep throat him. After plenty of this activity, Barry fucks me missionary style. Before he finishes, we fuck doggie style, too. That's when Barry loudly orgasms.

Barry had interrupted me during the early part of his fantasy to verbalize some of it himself. I thought, at the time, if this was his rudeness, it was not any big deal. Callers did it all the time. That was the only thing I noticed through his orgasm. However, as soon as his orgasm was finished, I found I was holding a dead phone. Barry had cum and gone.

Now, I knew where Barry had gotten his rude reputation. Yet, he was not the only man who had done this. There was a certain small percentage of callers who responded the same way. They came and they hung up. I found it annoying, just like anybody else who took calls. I ended up chatting with dead phones, as I did at the end of this call. I couldn't simply hang up because I wouldn't know why the caller had disappeared or even if he was returning. So, like anyone else who ever did phone sex fantasies, I continued talking about anything, until the phone disconnected us.

Barry had wanted a hot fantasy, which he got. I could only assume he enjoyed himself based on hearing his oral frenzy when he climaxed. Barry didn't save any money when he hung up on me, as he was charged ahead of time for a flat amount, and for a certain amount of time whether he used one minute or all of it. That's how it was done with the stars. I finally decided Barry was one of those guys who is speechless after getting off, too rattled to talk to anyone.

Continued from page 14

Occasionally, I used toys as props in photo shoots. They weren't always what a person would expect. For example, there was a photo of me in *Oui*
that was taken at the home of a former White House cook of Jackie Kennedy's.

In the photo I happened to be sucking on a huge Kohlrabi radish.

While dildos and vibrators are probably the most obvious and popular sexual toys, they are only the tip of the iceberg. The toys run the gamut from Ben Wa balls, a great toy for women, which have been around since ancient Japanese times, (and are still popular with women today), to electronic machines, for men's penises, which really do work. Accu-Jac was the one shown in my movie, *S.O.S.*

Most phallic-shaped items can be used as toys, but not all toys are penis-like. There are cock rings and butt plugs, French ticklers and scarves. Some men even use anatomically correct blowup dolls. Food items and spice-flavored body oils, or whips and handcuffs, sometimes add to the sexual action for people with those interests. The types and kinds of toys are endless, (and are extremely unusual in some cases), but if something can be used to enhance sexual acts it usually would be considered a toy, in that particular application.

Some of my callers would like to talk about sexual toys during our conversations. Sometimes, a caller would request I use a vibrator to which they could listen while we were talking. A certain number requested I use dildos.

Then, there were callers who liked to actually use toys themselves during the calls. A number of these callers would inform me that they already had toys connected to, or inserted in, their bodies before they were even on the phone with me.

On rare occasions I would get callers, who would tell me about unusual toys they were using during the call, with which I was not familiar. Those always made for interesting calls, especially if those items were intricate parts of their fantasies.

All the calls in this chapter involved toys, in some form or another. One of these calls did contain toys, which I did not recognize, although the caller assumed I was well-versed on all toys, by all names. Calls of this nature always demanded quick-wittedness on my part, and I did my best to fulfill their toy wishes!

CHAPTER 2

THE FANS

After I had been in erotica for a couple of years, I made one of my many lengthy visits to New York, for various career happenings; including the world premiere of one of my movies, doing interviews, shooting layouts, writing for magazines, discussing other movies with filmmakers, working on various projects, and making personal appearances.

While in New York, on this particular occasion, I was approached by an adult theatre, the Show World, about doing a stage show. Erotic film stars had not yet begun doing stage shows, at this time. The only exceptions were exotic dancers, who also eventually happened to make movies.

I was professionally trained in legitimate theatre, and I had acted in many plays, on stage, so the stage was not a foreign enemy to me. However, I had never been trained to be an exotic dancer, nor did I want to be. I told the theatre that wasn't my area of expertise. They asked me could I talk on stage. That would be easy for me, I said. They asked would I agree to briefly expose parts of myself to the audience. After giving it some thought, I said okay, as long as I didn't have to do a strip act. Additionally, I wouldn't get completely naked on stage, I told them.

The theatre and I worked out a plan where they would show one of my movies. Following the movie, I would come on stage, talk to the audience, tell humorous and sexy anecdotes, give brief glimpses of my more intimate body parts, including my jumping clit, but I would never get totally naked. I also would have a question and answer period with the audience in the last part of the show. Then, I would autograph my photos for fans.

I told the theatre I would like to start out this way, for the first day or two. If all went well, and I was comfortable, I was going to add some more sexy humor by bringing someone from the audience on stage. Excitedly, the manager asked what I had in mind for the customer. I could read his thoughts, and I cleared that up quickly. No, there would not be any hardcore action from me on stage. However, I was going to give the lucky audience member a thrill, by sucking his finger.

The manager looked at me as if I had lost my mind. He said to me, "This is New York, for crying out loud!"

I smiled at him, and said, "Yes, I know."

He added, "New Yorkers aren't going to go for that."

I remember I laughed, and said a couple of things. "You've never had your finger sucked by me, and I'll even sing a song on their fingers, and, then, I'll give them membership cards to my Finger Suckers' Club." I had started it a few years before in Kansas City.

The manager said, "Okay, go for it, but I bet you won't have any luck on stage with that, when these guys can go see live hardcore sex all over the street."

"You wait and see. Men will get excited!" I told him. "However, even if they don't, they'll have fun."

Thus, began my erotic stage show days. Only I didn't realize how it would evolve the day I signed my contract with the theatre.

Continued on page 34

Summer Phone Fling

Erotic film stars' fans are similar to all other kinds of entertainers' fans. They want to read about their stars, see them in films, on stage, or at personal appearances. These fans want autographs, photos, anything, relating to their stars. Occasionally, some of either kind of fans even think they are in love with their stars.

There can be a difference though. Sometimes, the erotic film stars' fans are fortunate enough to like a star who is doing phone sex calls. Then, those lucky fans might possibly call their stars.

Pete, from State College, Pennsylvania, was this kind of fan. He watched my movies. He saw me in magazines, and he decided he was in love.

The first time Pete called me he was a turned-on fan with a crush. The second time he called, he professed his love for me. He told me he was, initially, attracted by my looks, my long hair, and my oral abilities. Pete had also read my columns in a couple of men's magazines, and he said how much he loved a layout I had in another men's magazine. Although Pete kept saying he loved me throughout the call, he also mentioned a steady girlfriend, who was in Europe for the summer. He compensated for missing her by occasionally calling me.

Pete is into everything oral. He loves to have

me bend over so that he can lick my ass. Then, he loves to suck my nipples and lick my clit and pussy. Finally, he wants me to suck him off. During all this hot activity, he continuously tells me he loves me!

After Pete's horniness was satisfied, he begged me to meet him in Pittsburgh, Pennsylvania. Of course, I didn't agree to meet him, although he sounded like a really nice guy.

Pete had been the romantic-type caller. The romantic types were generally pleasant calls. Pete continued to stay romantic through all his calls with me.

* * * *

New York Groupie

Many professions attract groupies. Some, like professional athletes, rock stars, and high-level office holders, are especially notorious for that drawing power. Well, erotic film stars, have their share of groupies, too. I was no exception. I had my very own groupies, as well.

One groupie type, Eric, from New York City, called me regularly to chat, and to enjoy phone fantasy sex.

Eric, an electronics business owner, described himself as 6 feet 2 inches tall, 190 pounds, with graying hair and a mustache, and an "average" size penis. He indicated he was about forty years old.

When I talked with Eric, this particular August evening, he told me about some of the other erotic stars he had met, and, in some cases, how he had met them. He mentioned (the late) Jill Munro, a famous sex-change lady, who was well covered by **Cheri** magazine, when the magazine followed her through her change from male to female. He said he answered an ad and went to her apartment because she intrigued him.

Next, he mentioned a well-known East Coast star, Darby Lloyd Rains, who he also claimed to have met through some kind of advertisement. He had seen Darby in films and liked her.

Then, Eric told me he had gotten to know my friend and fellow erotic film star, Annie Sprinkle, by going to The Retreat in New York.

The Retreat was a very nice, extremely plush, massage parlor where Annie worked before getting involved in erotica, and, later, worked, again, occasionally for her own amusement and research.

Previous to me, Eric had talked with a few other xxx-rated film stars, I also found out during our chat. He had discovered that erotic film stars were a huge turn on for him. So, when he finally saw some of my movies, he became especially turned on to me.

At last, as we were getting into Eric's fantasy, he told me he didn't like anal sex. He said he was a leg man, with breasts coming in a high second. He mentioned he loved kissing, oral sex, and ears, as well. Eric said he loved tonguing women's ears and sucking their earlobes. He also stated he enjoyed to have his ass and testicles licked.

Eric's fantasy begins with the two of us on a date together. We have wine and dinner, and, then, he invites me to his place. After we arrive, he puts on music and fixes us drinks. He begins to seduce me by kissing me, and sharing tongues. He slowly unzips my dress and lightly touches my breasts, at the same time. Eric removes my dress. Then, he touches my hard nipples through my bra. My breasts fall forward as he removes my black satin bra. He gently grabs my breasts and massages them. Eric starts sucking my nipples, and, then, he licks my entire body, spending a lot of time on my legs. He puts his tongue in each of my ears and licks them, and sucks my earlobes, too. Then, Eric lays me back on the couch and he goes down on me. Eventually, he turns around. I lick his ass and testicles. I suck him. That is when he explodes in orgasm.

From my first call with Eric, it was clear to me he was very much attracted to erotic film stars. He would follow the careers of different ones, and attend any special appearances they made. He saw their movies. Eric would make every effort to meet them.

After Eric "discovered" me, he faithfully called me

every two weeks for years. He became attached to my career personality. He would seek out anything and everything pertaining to me, movies, stage shows, magazine stories and layouts, and personal appearances. For years, Eric constantly asked me to meet him in New York, and let him "please" me. I never did meet Eric, but I did remember him.

* * * *

Dallas Fan Club

One early September evening, I received a call from a twenty-two-year-old college student, and fan, named Dwayne. Dwayne, a new caller, from Dallas, told me he had begun a fan club for me there. He continued, saying that he had seen my spread in **High Society** magazine, and he had loved it! Dwayne also named several of my movies that he had enjoyed.

While conversing with Dwayne, I also learned he had participated in, and liked, group sex. In fact, he said he had gone to swingers' parties on several occasions. Furthermore, Dwayne said he loved oral sex. It was his very favorite sexual activity. He especially loved pleasing women orally. Dwayne told me he would very much enjoy pleasing me sexually in his fantasy.

In the phone fantasy, Dwayne comes to my hotel to talk to me about the fan club. While there, he expresses a desire to go down on me. I respond receptively to his request. We go to the bedroom and I allow him to remove my robe. I lie on the bed and he caresses my tits and briefly sucks them. Then, he slowly works his way down me until he reaches his favorite part of a woman. I spread my legs wide and he starts gently licking and nibbling on my pussy. He continues doing this and, suddenly, he climaxes while still at it.

It was obvious Dwayne really loved oral sex by his response to our conversation about it. After the sex part of the call, Dwayne also talked further about his fan club he had for me. I was certainly intrigued by that. He told me he would be calling me as often as could. He did continue calling me fairly regularly for about ten years.

The first couple of days, I did my show without anyone on stage, and the shows went very well. Fans brought me flowers and other goodies, and they returned for more shows. I came on stage to music, walked and danced around, waved to the fans, and showed, wiggled, and made "jump," what they wanted to see, as a warm up teaser. Then, I generally sat down in provocative positions and told sexy and funny tales about the x-rated movie industry, as well as other true adult stories. Sometimes I would walk around the stage while talking to the audience. Then, I took questions from the audience, which I thought was fun.

By the end of the second day, I was comfortable with my timing and their stage. So, then, I began asking for a volunteer after my anecdotes. I shortened the time for the anecdotes, as a result.

It was so easy getting volunteers, although they were clueless why I wanted them. I wouldn't tell ahead of time, either.

Initially, I had a washcloth on stage on the back of my chair, and I knew the volunteers had grand illusions of fulfilled fantasies. So, they were more than a little surprised, (after I teased them, and gave them an identify-the-body-parts test), when I took the washcloth and washed one of their fingers.

Then, I explained, and demonstrated, the techniques of cocksucking on their washed fingers, finishing it with singing and sucking some song, with lyrics and all, for which I was already famous worldwide.

The audience loved it! More interestingly, from the very beginning, the man on stage always really loved it. If an audience member didn't point it out, I would take a discreet look at his pants. If I notice a bulge, which I always did, then, I would have a little more verbal fun with the fellow. I never saw a guy upset over it. They enjoyed it, too.

After my first week of success, and the manager's total amazement at the audience's response, two things happened. More women and couples began attending my shows. The ladies wanted to learn more about oral sex. The guys would go home, and bring their women back with them. Sometimes, I would pick a couple to come on stage, and have her suck her man's other hand, and I would teach her what to do. It was one wild threesome!

The other thing that happened was during a show, one night, after I picked someone to come on stage. When the man arrived there, he asked what he was supposed to do. Jokingly, I said sit in a bowl of water. His response was, "Where's the bowl?" The audience thought it was hilarious.

The next day, I ran into Honeysuckle Divine, a famous stripper with her own unique act. I told her about the incident, and she said to me, "Jody, why don't you get a bowl and do that?"

Now, I was the one who thought she was crazy. However, Honeysuckle persuaded me to try it. She said just the idea of asking a guy to sit in it, should be very funny, and that I could wash his hand in it, at the least. Get a table and chairs, and a giant bowl, soap, water, some towels and go for it, she suggested.

Early the next day, I met with the manager, and told him I was going to make a few tiny changes in my show again. When I told him my plans, he said, "No way! No self-respecting New Yorker is going to sit in a bowl full of water on a table, on a stage in this city."

I said, "Wanna bet? And even if they don't, I can wash their hand and have fun with the idea of trying to persuade them. So it doesn't really matter."

He somewhat reluctantly agreed to get my stage set up, including providing me with a sturdy table, slightly smaller than a card table, and two chairs. I found the largest bowl in town and got the rest of my supplies. The stagehands had been told to fill the bowl with warm water for each show.

As I was about to go on stage for the first time with the bowl's presence, I noticed half the people who worked at that multi-floored complex were standing against walls and behind the audience, anywhere they could see, as the show was sold out. It was obvious that word had gotten out that Jody Maxwell was going to try something a little different. The manager was there watching, also.

The first "Bowl Show," as I called it, was going smoothly. Finally, I picked a volunteer from the audience, a nice looking fellow about thirty.

He came on stage and I did my usual confuse-the-person-on-stage, while identifying breasts, et cetera, routine. Then, when I felt he was warmed up and ready, I told him to sit in my bowl of water. The man almost fainted! He asked me to repeat my request.

With a totally straight face, I made my request again. The audience was loudly laughing. He asked me if I was serious. I told him, yes. He asked me about his pants. I said it didn't matter to me whether he left them on or took them off. He was very confused. I refused to say why I wanted him in the bowl.

That first time, I was secretly amazed, too, when suddenly the fellow took off his shoes, his nice, navy blue slacks, and his underwear, and stood there, blushing, in a dress shirt and black socks. Then, he stepped on a chair, onto the table, and gingerly put himself in the bowl.

Continued on page 43

Hot Super Fan

Sometimes, I received calls from fans, who had actually seen me, (or met me in person), on stage, at a premiere, or at a personal appearance. Those calls always seemed to add another dimension for these fans. Troy, from San Diego, was such a caller.

As a Teamsters Union Director, Troy frequently

had to make business trips, and some of those trips would take him to San Francisco, where I could often be found starring in a show at The Mitchell Brothers' O'Farrell Theatre.

Troy had been a longtime fan. He had seen lots of my movies, and had collected my magazines and layouts. When he had seen ads for my stage shows, he arranged to come see me. In fact, he said he had come to my shows several times. Since I starred in more than one show, at different times, at that theatre, I was curious which one he had seen.

My Kopenhagen Lounge show was the one to which he had kept returning. Troy confessed my shows made him so hot, that he had gone into the O'Farrell Theatre's men's room and had jerked off after the shows. He also admitted he had done the same thing to my layouts. He was totally fascinated that he was getting to talk to me one-on-one, privately. It was a fantasy-come-true in and of itself.

As excited as Troy was, he, also, had the presence of mind to ask me all kinds of questions about erotica. He wondered if I really got turned on doing my films, shows, or anything else I might have done in the world of erotica. Troy wanted to know if I had ever "swung." He asked me if I had ever dated a fan. Also, Troy was curious how I felt about my various directors, and about the different actors and actresses with whom I had worked. He had lots of questions. I answered as many as I could or would.

Abruptly, Troy changes directions and tells me he wants to fuck me, and he wants me to wear stockings and hi heels while we are doing it. He lies back, and asks me to get on top of him so he could lick my breasts dangling in his face, while we are screwing. Then, he desires for me to pull off him, and suck him until he cums. Troy cums hard in his phone fantasy.

Fans like Troy were always fun because they were so happy getting to talk to me. I enjoyed talking to them because I knew I was giving them something extra special by which to remember me. I always looked forward to hearing from my super fans, and that certainly included Troy.

* * * *

Panties For Sale

Sometimes, I received calls from hardcore fans that were so enamored of me, that they would initially have trouble talking. So, I would do small talk with them until they calmed down and were ready to chat with me.

One such caller was Tim, from Boston, who said he was an attorney. Tim told me he normally wasn't speechless, but he was momentarily stunned by getting to talk to me after all the years he had been reading about me in magazines, and watching me in movies. Tim said the moment he heard my voice he knew it was really I.

Now, Tim was happy, and wanted to talk about how he found himself captivated by me. He said he had a lot of fantasies involving me, including some he hoped he could actually fulfill. These included wanting most of all to buy my panties. Tim didn't care what they cost, as long as they were mine, and that I had worn them. Additionally, he very much wanted to join my fan club. Tim desired autographed photos, too. He wanted anything connected with me.

After Tim completed his wish list, it was time for him to be thinking about his phone fantasy with me. I knew in some ways it was already completed for him, by just having our conversation. However, I realized he wanted to take it further than that.

Tim tells me he has a heated waterbed, and he very much dreams of me being on it with him. So, that is where his phone fantasy sex takes place. We are lying in bed, kissing. Then, I move down his body and in between his legs. I start sucking him, and, at his request, I do some of the famous techniques I had previously created. When he thinks he is getting too hot from that, he decides we should change places, and he goes down on me. Finally, he lies back on the bed and has me fuck him with me on top so he can suck my tits, at the same time. He cums while we are fucking.

Tim loved his phone fantasy sex and he loved the non-sexual part of the conversation, too. He still wanted to buy whatever he could from me, but wanted my panties most of all.

I enjoyed talking to Tim. It was always fun to talk to someone who was such a huge fan. The big fans seemed so happy and pleased to converse with me, it always made me feel good. Besides, in Tim's case, he was such a courteous guy as well as a devoted fan, I couldn't help but like him. I hoped to talk with him again.

* * * *

Minneapolis Moments

It was always fun to receive calls from true fans, and to hear what they had to say. It gave me a chance to better know some of my regular fans, and it gave them the opportunity to really talk to me.

I accepted such a call, one evening, from Alex, in Minneapolis. Alex had been my fan since he saw my very first movie, and he had followed my career through the years. As an executive with a major food manufacturer, Alex traveled all over and had seen me on stage on both coasts, as well as seeing my movies and reading my magazine columns. So, he was pretty excited when he got me on the phone.

Early in the conversation, Alex described himself as being 6 feet tall, weighing about 175 pounds, with blondish-brown hair and green eyes. He said he thought he was pretty well built. He, also, told me he was an alcoholic, but had not had a drink in years.

Alex continued talking, saying that his favorite part of a woman was her mouth. He said I had a beautiful mouth, made for kissing. He told me that he loved oral sex, "giving head and getting head," as he put it. He thought oral sex was the perfect foreplay to "good fucking."

Following that, Alex told me he had been watching a porn movie, unfamiliar to me, when he called. However, he didn't call to have phone sex. He just wanted to talk to me. Alex mentioned how much he enjoyed sex and had been swinging for several years, and loved it! He went into details about swingers' clubs in the greater Minneapolis area. Alex definitely sounded knowledgeable on the subject!

Finally, it was time to say goodbye to Alex. I had enjoyed his easy-going style, his great attitude, and certainly all his compliments. He definitely had been a fun fan and a fun call.

Continued from page 37

The sight was awesome! This good-looking man was sitting in a bowl full of water, on a table, facing the audience, trying to keep the tails of his shirt dry. He couldn't move, either, because he was all the way down in the bowl, with his legs hanging over the front of the bowl.

I heard later the audience was laughing so loud that security came up to see what was going on. A couple of New York's finest were passing through, as well, so, they also, came to see my very first bowl show. I was told they thought it was great!

It was truly an astonishing sight. I managed to not break up, although it was difficult being straight. I then got the washcloth and washed his finger, on which I sucked and sang, while he sat in the bowl.

There was one other interesting effect I hadn't thought about ahead of time. My bowl person got an erection while I was sucking his finger, and suddenly the "head" popped up above the bowl.

People were literally rolling in the aisles. Thus, was born my "Bowl Show."

Getting him out of the bowl was challenging but worked out okay. He was thrilled about getting his finger sucked, although I felt certain he would have preferred something else sucked. He got dried off and dressed, and the audience gave him a standing ovation. I gave the bowl man a nice 8 x 10 autographed photo and a free pass to another show.

The next morning, the florist delivered yellow

roses from him, with a note telling me it was the most exciting moment of his life!

After the first bowl show, people would make friendly wagers about following shows, whether or not I could get the next person in the bowl. I stayed away from the betting because I simply was not concerned one way or another. I had created it so it worked either way, in or out. However, I always succeeded in getting the guy in the bowl, so those who bet on me were doing well.

I began to think of the guys as my "bowl people," and as belonging to an exclusive club. I respected and admired their gutsiness. Many of them told me, later, that they felt they could do most anything after sitting in the bowl.

The number of women attending my shows kept increasing. The dancers would watch my shows when they had a chance. In the dressing room, it would get pretty funny because all the dancers would come to me to teach them sucking techniques on their fingers. A stagehand came in to bring me a message one evening, and there were about five girls sucking their fingers and trying out techniques at the time. He took one look at the activities and actually ran from the room, obviously, freaked out.

Due to the show's success I began booking it in other cities throughout the country. Over and over, I would be told nobody is going to sit in a bowl of water on a table, on stage. Over and over, everybody sat in the bowl of water on stage, no matter where I was appearing. I probably had no more than five people, total, in the years I did my Bowl Show, who did **not** sit in the bowl.

Of course, there were always interesting and unexpected occurrences when dealing with mystery guests on stage. I was in Iowa, doing the show, during a below freezing blizzard. Due to the weather I figured it would be difficult to get people into the bowl. During my first show at this engagement, a very nice, guy came on stage, dressed in layers. He said he was twenty-eight years old. I did my usual banter with him and finally got down to the big question about sitting in the bowl. This fellow wasn't thrilled with the idea, initially, but, with persuasion, he agreed, and he actually was getting enthused about it.

First, he needed to remove some clothing, starting with his coat. He continued taking off articles of clothing and his boots. Finally, he was down to his shirt and jeans. When he took them off, too, I even lost my deadpan expression. He was wearing one-piece long johns, standing on my stage, with back flap and all.

When the audience stopped laughing, he pointed out to me if he removed his long johns he was going to be naked. Somehow I had already figured that out. I told him he could sit in the water in his long johns but he would get frost-butt when he wore them wet outside later, or he could get naked.

The fellow decided naked was better. So, he removed his socks and the long johns, then, sat totally naked in the bowl on a bone-freezing day. Although I prided myself on my straight face abilities, this guy got to me, and broke me up.

Continued on page 56

Erotic Film Dancer

Some guys enjoyed talking with erotic film stars. They would find out which few did fantasy phone sex calls and, then, see their movies. If the men liked the movies, they would call the stars. One of the men who found pleasure in this preparation was Jarrod, who called me very late one night, from Anchorage, Alaska.

Jarrod, who said he worked for the federal government, had a pleasant voice, and seemed very nice. He talked about what it was like to live in Alaska, which was interesting to me, since it was the only state that I had never visited.

After this brief chat, Jarrod mentioned matters of a more sexual nature. He told me he was fond of a little domination, cocksucking, lingerie, and hi heels. Then, Jarrod shared his lifelong ambition, as he referred to it, to make love to a dancer. The perfect dancer, in his mind, was a woman who also was an erotic film star.

He had previously read about my various kinds of shows, including one where I did do some dancing.

This had put his fantasy thoughts in motion. Since Jarrod had already seen some of my movies, he was happy I could do sexy, sensual dancing, as well.

Jarrod's phone sex fantasy takes place in the Kopenhagen Lounge at O'Farrell Theatre in San Francisco. In his fantasy, he places himself in the audience in this lovely, plush, scarlet-red and gold, mirrored room. I am starring in a show in there.

I come out in a dark silver-blue silk and lace, sequin-trimmed, long gown, slit up the middle to just the top of my thighs. I have on long, black, sheer stockings and five-inch, black, slinky hi heels.

As Jarrod's fantasy continues, I dance slowly, seductively for the audience. I come up very close to the individuals in the audience for fleeting seconds, while continuously dancing. I do some fancy moves that Jarrod finds extremely exciting.

Finally, I dance close to Jarrod, in his fantasy. Only this time, I lightly brush myself against him, and then, unexpectedly, I reach out and grab his erect penis through his pants while continuing doing little dance moves. Then, I unzip his pants, and I kneel in front of him and suck him briefly, while rubbing my barely-covered breasts on his testicles. Following that, I stand up, remove my panties, and spread my legs, on the outside of his, and bend my knees, in an almost straddling position, so that my clitoris barely touches the tip of his penis. I continue to move rhythmically to my music.

After some of this teasing, I slowly straddle myself more on Jarrod's penis, as he enters me, and we begin fucking. I manage to turn myself around while continuously sitting on his penis so I am facing outward with my back to him, as if I am simply sitting on his lap. Jarrod is fucking me hard, now, in his fantasy.

Finally, Jarrod asks me to suck him off. So I get up, and, again, kneel in front of him, and go back to sucking. In his fantasy, he wants to cum on my tongue, while I am sticking it out. I fulfill his wish. Jarrod has an immense orgasm.

Jarrod was an interesting fan, who liked to make his phone sex fantasies closer to three dimensional, by watching my films, and checking out magazine stories on me. He essentially did his homework before calling, to see if he felt some form of compatibility with his fantasy and me together. He was very happy with his assessment!

* * * *

Presidential Chat

I always enjoyed it when really big fans called. So, I was certainly pleased when the screener phoned me to say that the president of a Phoenix area fan club of mine, wanted to have a call with me. The screener said his name was Derek and he seemed very friendly.

Derek began the conversation by telling me how he started my fan club chapter, after he saw my first erotic film, **Portrait**. Since then, he had seen all my movies, read everything I had written, and had a collection of my photos and layouts. He also shared these various things with fellow members.

Following the fan club talk, Derek told me he was twenty-three years old, and had recently broken up with his girlfriend. He said he was a graduate student at the University of Arizona, and that he was a bouncer at a nightclub in the evenings. Derek talked about the college girls he had been picking up lately, at work and at school, since he was a free man again.

He also proudly told me he had a straight 8-inch cock, and he loved to eat pussy. While Derek made it clear he just wanted to talk and not have fantasy phone sex with me, he did say his longtime, ultimate fantasy was for me to sing a song on his cock. He said he had dreamed of this for years.

There were lots of questions on Derek's mind. He wanted to know my favorite color, favorite sports, and what kind of music I liked. Naturally, Derek had lots of questions about my taste in men. He asked for the details of my first kiss, and about my romances in high school and college. Derek requested that I describe the perfect man. Some questions, like that one, were difficult to answer. Others were very easy.

Derek had lots of questions about swinging, as well. Since I had frequently written about swinging clubs throughout the country, he was extremely curious about the tidbits I may not have mentioned in my writings. He was also anxious to find out what it would take for him to get a membership in one of these clubs.

Finally, it was time for Derek and me to say our goodbyes. He said how much he greatly appreciated the privilege of talking with me, and that he was thrilled he would be able to call me on more occasions.

From my point of view, Derek was very nice, and I enjoyed talking with him. It was a relaxing, laid-back, pleasant call. I thought it would be fun if he called again. As it turned out, he called many times over the next few years.

* * * *

Prescription for Pleasure

Some callers had desires that were unique from what they felt they could do in their real lives. They wanted to do various things considered a little off-the-wall by the so-called normal standards. These callers sometimes were in positions in their communities where they thought that any knowledge of their secret lusts could be detrimental to their careers. Frequently, they were probably correct to be concerned.

During my years in erotica, I became aware that huge numbers of people added their own special touches to their most personal fantasies, but I also discovered that most people were not ready to publicly accept anything but the considered "norm" from their fellow members of society. So, anyone of stature usually had good reason to be apprehensive about his or her secret wants.

One such caller, Brandon, from Roanoke, Virginia, was a forty-eight-year-old pharmacist, and prominent Roanoke citizen, who described himself as standing 5 feet 11 inches, and weighing 155 pounds. He had gray hair and brown eyes.

Immediately, Brandon told me he had been a major, long time fan, and he had even made a special trip from Virginia, to see me live, on stage, in Pittsburgh, Pennsylvania. He said he loved my show, and that I autographed a photo for him afterward. Brandon also mentioned he was crazy about my face and my "derriere."

After commenting on my career and me, Brandon talked about how he adored women, in general, and he especially loved to please them. He referred to himself as a "crazy fetishist" because his desire to please women reached a certain level where he liked being in a slave-type role to women in dominant roles. He said one of his favorite fantasies was having a threesome with a "dyke-mistress," (his word), and another woman, and the women using strapped-on dildos on each other and on him. Brandon added he was also was into toe sucking.

Of course, I figured all that he had mentioned was in his phone sex fantasy, but Brandon actually had something else in mind that night. He said because he was excited to be talking to me, he wanted just the two of us doing the things he had in mind.

Brandon's fantasy begins with the two of us in my hotel room following my performance. He wants me to tie him up with my stockings I wore during my stage show. I tie him spread eagle on my bed. Then, he wishes to be teased.

I do a sensuous strip for him, taking off my dress and my bra. I leave on my black silk panties. I straddle his naked body, but do not intimately touch him. I slap him in the face with my tits and then I dangle my tits in his face for him to try and catch with his tongue. He gets a few licks in, but misses a lot. I sit on his cock with my panties on, so he cannot penetrate me. It drives him crazy.

Then, I move up his body rubbing my covered pussy along his stomach and chest. I almost, but not quite, sit on his face. He stretches his tongue out so that he can feel my clit through the silk panties.

He wants to sniff my panties, so I make him pull them off with his teeth. He finally gets them off. I put my panties on his nose and tell him to deeply sniff them. After that, I offer my panties to his mouth and tell him to chew on the crotch. Next, I take my panties and put one leg opening over his cock and balls and leave them there for the rest of his phone sex fantasy.

Now, he gets to actually suck my tits as I offer them one at a time to his lips. When my nipples are totally hard I rub them down his body and all over his cock. Following that, I move back up again to his face and have him lick my pussy. When I decide there's been enough pussy licking, I go down him and suddenly put little kisses all over his cock and balls. I act like I am going to suck him but only give him flashes of my lips wrapped around his cock, in his fantasy. Also, I lick his cock, until he begs me to suck him.

After briefly sucking him, he again begs me. This time he pleads for me to sit on his cock, with my panties, of course, still attached to him. Finally, I do sit on his cock and fuck him. He explodes inside me.

When Brandon calmed down, after cumming, he wanted to chat for a short while longer. He told me he had seen three other erotic film stars on stage over the years, but that I was definitely his all-time favorite. He also mentioned the impossibility of fulfilling his fantasies at home. At last, when we said goodbye, I knew I would be hearing from Brandon again.

Brandon was a nice guy, who liked to do all kinds of sexy things, in which the woman was the boss and he was there to please her. It was an exciting call and he was one hot man. I wondered what we would do next time he called.

* * * *

Attorney Career Change

In the wee hours, one May morning, I received a call from an Austin, Texan, named Andre, a new Personal Services Club member. Initially, Andre acted a little nervous, but I soon put him at ease. Andre was 27 years old, 5 feet 11 inches tall, 165 pounds, with thinning brown hair, and hazel eyes. He had seen several of my movies; however, his all time favorite was **Expose Me Lovely.**

Andre said he was a graduate of the University of

Texas, and played college football there. Now, he was a young, single, corporate trial lawyer.

As Andre began to open up, he told me he had a 6-inch cock, and that he loved tits, especially big tits. He claimed his favorite sexual activity was pussy eating. Andre sounded like he was about to get into a phone sex fantasy, but that wasn't the case.

He was more interested in talking to me about the world of erotica, than fulfilling any fantasy. Andre had lots of questions too. He discussed some of my scenes in my movies, wondering how complex it was to shoot some of the hotter ones. He asked me about my co-stars, both male and female. Andre was curious how I saw them, as actors or lovers. There were lots of questions regarding sex scenes, including how long specific scenes took to film, what were "fluffers," what were "loops," and were there always multiple cameras used, among others. Andre wondered how much the directors called the shots in the sex scenes. He even asked about the male actors' stamina.

Then, Andre wanted to know how actors and actresses get into the business, and whether it was hard to break into the world of erotic films. He asked what the difference was between West Coast and East Coast erotica, and the people in it, or if there was any difference.

Finally, Andre told me his real fantasy was to be in erotic films and loops. He said he thought about it a lot. He would want to be disguised somehow because of his law career, but Andre wanted to do sex scenes with superlative lovers in front of a camera. He didn't care about doing the acting, he only wanted to be a sex performer or a "body." Andre wanted to be admired for his sexual prowess by millions of horny people.

I gave Andre some suggestions how he could possibly get some auditions, if that was really his wish. I warned him, though, that there was more to it than just getting naked with a bunch of beautiful women. That did not dampen his enthusiasm at all.

When the call ended, Andre was very nice and thanked me for our pleasant conversation. He said he would call again. As a final gesture before saying goodbye, he taught me his alma mater's "Hook 'Em Horns" sign. I did hear from Andre a bunch of times over the next few years.

Continued from page 45

Actually, to my astonishment, everybody at that engagement sat in the bowl. I had the theatre keep the stage a little too warm, so that it was easier for the potential bowl people to decide what to do.

Another thing that occasionally occurred during my engagements was the man would decide either to sit in the bowl with his underwear on, or even wearing all his clothing. That never bothered me. After all, it was very funny, dressed, as well, but I always wondered how they physically felt in their wet clothing afterward.

My show, while extremely funny, was also sexy, sensuous, and erotic. I had always been a firm believer that sex could be beautiful and hot, and yet have humor in it, too. With this show I fulfilled the audience's desires to see some nudity and sexiness, imparted them with knowledge on improving their sex lives, presented them with humor, and showed them the possibilities of getting turned on while laughing, too.

I did suspect that some of them felt grateful they were not among the chosen. While I think this, I know many men came up to me over the years and said how much they envied the guy in the bowl, and wished they had been picked.

My fan base grew larger with every stage appearance. I would hear from both men and women telling me how much they enjoyed the show. One man, who sat in the bowl, even surprised me later with a beautiful 16 by 20 inch canvas portrait painting he did of me because he found it the most exhilarating experience of his life!

Of course, by the time I began doing fantasy phone sex calls, my fan base came from many sources throughout the world, as well as my stage shows. Frequently, I would receive calls from fans of my Bowl Show, (audience and participants), or fans of mine for other reasons, such as, my films, layouts, columns and writings, personal appearances, my other kinds of shows, and so on.

Talking with my fans was a delight. They always

seemed happy to have the opportunity to chat with me. However, just because the callers were fans, it did not mean I could assume what the subjects or types of the calls would be. Naturally, some of my fans would want fantasy phone sex, but many simply wanted the opportunity to just talk with me, as if we were long-time friends. Others would ask me questions about myself and my world, to which they didn't know the answers. A lot of those callers seemed to be pleased to play the interviewer for a change.

My fans would call and share their own personal, private moments with me, too, and would sometimes even ask for advice on virtually any subject, not just sex.

The fan calls were always fascinating because I never knew if they were going to be hot and heavy or sweet and sentimental, erotic or G-rated. I only knew I thought they were great calls.

Continued on page 66

Just Chit-Chat

During my first two weeks receiving calls, I talked to all kinds of men with all kinds of sexual fantasies. Then, I spoke with Joseph, from St Louis. He was quite a bit different from all the previous calls I'd had, to that point.

Joseph was extremely pleasant and very nice. He described himself as a 6-foot-7-inch, 270-pound accountant in his thirties. He made it clear that he simply wanted to visit with me, and to tell me he enjoyed my writings and my movies. Joseph said that he was impressed with my looks and my intelligence. That's why he called, he stated. Clearly, he did not want phone sex.

I enjoyed chatting with Joseph. He talked to me about career-related things I should and should not do regarding taxes. Joseph asked me what other various erotic stars were like, not sexually, but as real people. There were lots of questions from Joseph, but none of them pertained to sex. He inquired about my college days and my theatrical acting. Naturally, he was curious about the erotic film business, but his questions were more about me, similar to what a regular interviewer might ask. He even asked me to describe what would be a typical outfit for me to wear out on a regular casual, non-working day. There wasn't any phone fantasy sex with Joseph, just two people visiting.

It was fun and easy to talk with Joseph. I took his reason for calling at face value. If he was calling because he was feeling lonely, I really didn't know. It was not apparent in our conversation. He did not speak as if he were nervous or apprehensive, only like an old friend who had been away. When the call ended I knew I would look forward to hearing from Joseph again.

* * * *

Vancouver Small Talk

Shep called me one evening from Vancouver, in Canada. He sounded friendly, pleasant, and talkative. He immediately told me he was involved with international championship auto shows and was enjoying a small break. Shep continued to talk about his career, and his own collection of fancy vehicles. We also compared notes on people we both knew in that business. Abruptly, Shep asked me if he could call me back in a couple of minutes because his roommate had just come in.

About three minutes later, Shep was back on the phone, apologizing for the interruption. This time,

I figured, he'd want to talk about sex. However, I was wrong. Now, he asked me about my friend, Rita Ricardo, whom he had seen on stage there, in Vancouver. He commented that she seemed like a nice girl. He didn't say anything sexy about Rita or others. He just did not seem to want to go in that direction.

Then, Shep asked me about my live stage shows. He had seen me in magazines and movies, but not my shows, and he was curious. I told him about my basic, and somewhat unusual, stage show, that I had done from coast to coast. I also told him about my other show, which I created for the Kopenhagen Lounge at The O'Farrell Theatre in San Francisco. Although he asked questions about the shows, they were not sexual questions.

When the time limit had been reached, Shep told me how much he enjoyed talking with me and that he hoped we would get a chance to visit again. I could tell he was genuinely sincere. He really had enjoyed just chit-chatting.

I knew Shep hadn't had a sexual experience, but I also knew he didn't call for one. He simply wanted to talk to me, which he did. Was he simply a fan? I had no idea, although my thoughts leaned in that direction. I did know, though, that people called erotic film stars, such as myself, for many reasons other than sex.

Shep's call was a good example of what was known as a "straight" call. He was a nice guy, and I looked forward to hearing from him again.

People called fantasy phone sex clubs for many reasons, not always for the obvious ones. The reasons people called erotic film stars at these numbers could be even more varied because the callers frequently were familiar with the stars they were calling.

* * * *

Jody's Therapeutic Call

Early one evening I received a call from Milt, a bachelor, who lived in an upper scale St. Louis suburb. Milt, in his early thirties, with dark blonde hair and baby blue eyes, was the Chief Financial Officer at a large, high-powered real estate firm. I had talked to Milt on previous occasions and had found him to be a pleasant, decent, sensitive guy. It was always nice to hear from him.

Milt never desired fantasy phone sex when he called, but only wanted to chat with me. This time was no different. He reminded me that he liked to talk about me, and to me, as a person, not as a star. This time, he had several topics on his mind.

He wanted to know if I could cook, and what some of my favorite dishes to cook were. Milt was pleased I enjoyed cooking because he loved to eat. He wistfully told me that I should cook for him sometime.

After discussing some Cheese Balls recipes from

one of our mutually favorite cookbooks, Milt went to his next topic. He was curious about the kind of men I had dated. He didn't ask the sexual questions, but more innocuous ones. Did I have a "type" I preferred, in looks, education, careers, mannerisms. Milt asked me to tell him about some of the fellows, who I had really enjoyed dating.

When that topic had been covered enough for this call, Milt asked if he could discuss with me, a personal problem he was having. He spoke of an underlying depression he had been suffering for the last few months. Milt talked about being troubled and not knowing why. I felt badly for him, so, I let him continue.

When he was finished with as much as he wished to say, I encouraged Milt to go to a professional, who could hopefully determine the source of his problem.

Finally, Milt told me about a place where he loved to drive near the Mississippi River, and watch the sunrise, when the weather was nice. He found tranquility and beauty there. He told me I reminded him of that sunrise. I made him feel good, he said.

As the call ended, I noticed that Milt seemed more cheerful and energized than he had been at the beginning of the call. I hoped talking with me really did help, since he certainly sounded better. Most of all, I wanted him to seek out a medical professional to get his problem resolved.

* * *

Not for Sale

    Sal, from Philadelphia, called me very late one night, really excited that he actually was getting to talk to me. He had been at the world premiere of my movie, **Portrait**, in Philadelphia, and had been a super fan ever since.

    Sal told me he was the thirty-nine-year-old owner of a large limousine service. As far as his looks were concerned, Sal said he had black, piercing eyes, and dark brown curly hair. He weighed about 205 pounds and was 6 feet 2 inches tall. Further, Sal said he was very muscular, but that his biggest muscle was his cock. It was apparent he was very proud of how well endowed he was. He claimed he had never met a girl who could suck his cock "all the way" because it was much too big, in both length and width. Just once in his life, Sal wished a girl could suck him the way he surmised normally endowed men got sucked. This was Sal's big dream. Sal did have one other dream though, he told me.

    He very much wanted to make a movie with me. He had fantasized doing that ever since he first saw me in Philadelphia for my movie's premiere. If he couldn't do that, then, he wished to get it on with me just once before he died. He continued, telling me he was single, on his own, and was wealthy.

Next, Sal told me he was crazy about my breasts. He thought they were perfect and natural. He said sometimes he dreamed about sucking them. Sal absolutely wanted to bury his head in my breasts.

As I listened to Sal, I was beginning to assume that his phone sex fantasy was going to involve oral sex and my breasts, but that was not where he was headed. Sal had bigger plans than that.

At this point, Sal made it clear he didn't want to have phone sex with me. He had other ideas. He wanted to spend one hour with me, in person, in the flesh. He mentioned his single status and wealth again. Then, he started off by offering me $500. for that one hour, and all expenses, of course. All I could do was laugh. Sal thought I meant that amount was unacceptable. He increased it to $1000. I laughed some more because I couldn't believe he really thought he could buy an hour with me. Well, my laughing raised it to $2000. Pretty soon, the amount was $5000., or any larger amount I determined for his one special hour.

Of course, I never even considered such an offer. Although Sal sounded like a nice guy, I was not for sale, nor for rent, for one hour or even for one minute. While I was a star in the world of erotica, I was still my own person.

I very nicely explained this to Sal, and although he was obviously extremely disappointed, he took it graciously. He asked me when and where I expected to do my next super-sexy, stand-up comedy show, and if he could come and see it. I told him he was welcome to see my shows any time he wished.

Sal did call me a few more times to chat, but he never mentioned paying me to spend an hour with him again. However, Sal was not the only man over the years, who offered me money like that. There were many who did and I unanimously turned them down.

Continued from page 58

Some fans were regular and frequent callers, (including a number of my Bowl Show fans), over the years. They called strictly because they were fans, and always enjoyed the prospect of getting to talk one-on-one with me in any possible way. I was always pleased to hear from those fans because I felt I had gotten to know them through their calls.

I found calls with my fans were always entertaining, whether they called one time or one hundred times. Whatever their reasons for being my fans, I definitely always enjoyed their calls.

CHAPTER 3

SWINGING DAYS

While swinging has been around forever, contemporary swinging began its upsurge in the late 1960's, reaching its golden era in the 70's through the early 80's.

I personally became aware of swinging, up close, in the early 70's, when my boyfriend and I first decided to try it out on a spur of the moment after a night on the town. The opportunity presented itself, so we went for it. While some couples go out to breakfast after an evening of partying, we had breakfast in bed that night. Initially, it was only with one other couple. Yet, we found the experience stimulating, so decided to do a little exploring of this whole new world.

John, my boyfriend, and I thought we were getting involved in high adventure, and in many ways we were. This was the beginning of our safari into the sexual, swinging jungle.

After our virgin escapade, we began talking to some of our friends about swinging, but not all, of course. Since we were both divorced, by then, that was not an encumbrance. However, we were each known and respected in our home community. He was president of his own company, and I was still in college, but heavily involved in the Republican Party, including holding party offices, at that very same time. I was engaged in other community activities, as well. Plus, I came from a prominent midwestern family. So, John and I had to be somewhat discreet with whom we shared this other side of our lives.

Nevertheless, in our conversations we did have about swinging, with friends and other people, I discovered that a high percentage of men fantasized about being with two women at the same time, which is generally considered a type of swinging. These were not exclusive **Playboy** or **Penthouse Forum** fantasies. These were the things a great number of real men actually thought about – the threesome.

Continued on page 75

Ultimate Caribbean Cruise

Frequently, I would hear from callers in Ft. Worth, Texas. One of those callers was Howard, who described himself as in his early thirties, with dark blonde hair, blue eyes, a nice body, and about 5 feet 11 inches tall. Howard told me he was a married executive with a large international company, and that he drove a Trans Am. Next to sex, Howard loved classic cars, and was proud of his collection, he said.

Howard was a fan of mine, as I had discovered in previous calls with him. He had seen several of my movies, and layouts, ands had read my magazine columns, over the years. Now, he was ready for his latest fantasy involving me. This one combined some reality with his fantasy.

The reality was that Howard and his wife were leaving on a cruise in a couple of months, traveling through the entire Caribbean. The fantasy part was that Howard wanted me to join him and his wife, Jeannie, on the cruise.

Howard's fantasy phone sex begins with the three of us settling in on the ship. Then, we go on deck, admire the view, and make small talk. After that, we head for the lounge where we have pitchers of Margaritas, and do some dancing. At some point, we decide to head for the cabin. We

have a beautiful VIP cabin, which is fairly large for a cruise ship.

Jeannie, a slender, leggy brunette, with large breasts, has been rubbing up against me all night. Howard loves it. For his part, he has been sticking his tongue in my ear throughout the evening.

We arrive at our cabin, carrying another pitcher of Margaritas. After we get inside, Jeannie and Howard immediately come kiss me, at the same time, back and forth.

Then, Howard removes my blouse, and plays with my breasts through my blue satin bra. Meanwhile, Jeannie takes off my skirt. She is rubbing her hands all over the lower half of my body. Howard pulls me to the bed, and lays me back on it. During this, Jeannie is undressing. When she gets completely naked, she comes over and lies down next to me. Jeannie removes my bra and starts sucking my breasts. Howard watches for a moment as he undresses. Then, he pulls off my blue silk panties, and begins to eat me, while Jeannie continues to suck my nipples.

About then, Howard, turns around so we can "69." Jeannie moves up and we suck Howard's cock together while he continues to eat me until I climax in his fantasy. Howard is so turned on by me getting off, he wants to fuck me. Immediately, he takes me while I am lying on my back. Jeannie kisses her husband as he continues fucking me missionary style. Then, she puts her pussy next *to my face, wanting me to go down on her, while Howard and I are fucking.*

Howard wants to change positions, so Jeannie pulls away. He lies back on the bed and I get on top of him. Jeannie goes down and licks both of us as he goes in and out of me.

Now, Howard wants to do it doggie style. He pulls out, turns me around, and gets me on my hands and knees. He spreads my legs apart, puts his head between them and eats me, again. His tongue is very active over the entire area. Jeannie is briefly sucking her husband's cock while his busy mouth and tongue are working on me.

Finally, Howard fucks me doggie style, and Jeannie French-kisses me, at the same time. When Howard is on the verge of cumming, he pulls out and quickly gets his cock in my mouth. He has me suck him in the fantasy until he cums that way. Then, Jeannie kisses me again, immediately after her husband has cum.

Following his orgasm, Howard talked some more about their cruise, but he told me the cruise just wouldn't be the same without me. It was a brief chat, at the end of the call, since Howard was having difficulty staying awake because he was so drained and relaxed. After we hung up, I had a feeling I would hear from Howard, again, before he left on the cruise.

* * * *

Calgary Threesome

I always enjoyed receiving calls from my fans North of the border. They were generally eager for some kind of a sexual adventure in their fantasies. Wade from Calgary, Alberta, Canada, who called late one night, was no exception.

Before we got to his fantasy, Wade told me he was a professional sportsman. Hunting and fishing were his fields. Wade stated he was in excellent physical condition because of his work, and that he was a blue-eyed, blonde stud.

Wade told me he had seen me in various magazines, including **Cheri**, **Hustler**, **Escapade**, and **High Society**, among others, and had been entertained by reading my columns in a couple of them. He had found me to be a sexy, sensual, hot babe, who turned him on in many ways. While he was offering his compliments, he added that he loved my shapely breasts, and that he was a big tit man.

I could tell it was time for Wade's phone sex fantasy. He knew exactly what he wanted in his fantasy, too. Wade desired a three-some composed of him, his girlfriend, Karen, and me. It was to take place in his queen-sized bed in his home.

The fantasy begins with the three of us already in bed. He and Karen, a well-endowed, pretty brunette, are naked. I am still dressed as I am the "honored" guest. They are making out, deep kissing and touching each other. I sit on the bed and watch. Then, Wade and Karen come over to me and they both give me a kiss with lots of tongue.

After the tongue kissing, they slowly undress me. Wade and Karen caress me as they remove my clothing. When they take off my sheer red bra, they each gently take one of my breasts and suck it, as they lay me back on the bed. With one of them on each side of me they finish undressing me. At the same time, they continue fondling and sucking my breasts.

Next, Wade comes up and straddles my chest, and sticks his hard cock between my breasts. When he does this, I squeeze my breasts around his cock allowing him to fuck them. Meanwhile, Karen spreads my legs apart as she uses her tongue on my pussy. Wade moves further up me and sticks his throbbing cock into my mouth. He has me suck him in this position. At the same time, we can tell Karen is turned on by my pulsating clit, as we both hear her moan how much she loves it.

Now, Wade lies back on the bed, and Karen and I go down on him together. She licks his balls while I suck his cock. Then, she comes up

Wade is rock hard. He reaches for Karen, who sits on his face, while I continue to suck him. He's in seventh heaven feeling my lips wrapped around his cock, while his own lips are on his girlfriend's delicious pussy.

At this point, Wade wishes to fuck Karen and me. I stop sucking, while Karen sits on his cock. She leans forward and he sucks her large tits, and I suck them with him. Suddenly, Karen cums hard, and falls off him in exhaustion. Wade still wants a little more. So he has me lie on my back and he fucks my tight, juicy pussy. Wade grabs my legs, and raises them as high as his neck, so he can deep stroke me. He is fucking me hard and fast, now. Wade tells me to cum. Abruptly, he yells out that he's cumming inside my pussy.

Following Wade's fantastic orgasm, he was virtually too numb to immediately speak. I listened to him pant as he was regaining his breath. Finally, when he was able to talk, he told me how much he enjoyed his phone sex fantasy and he could hardly wait to tell his girlfriend about it, when she returned from visiting relatives in Great Britain. He also asked if they could call me together some time. Of course, the answer was yes.

Wade was a lot of fun and wildly hot. I wondered what his next call would be like. There was one thing for certain, it would be another sexual adventure.

Continued from page 68

John and I were slowly making our way along the jungle trail. We experimented with some threesome situations. Since it was the era of female liberation, and he was a fair-minded guy, we checked out both ways, two females or two males to make a threesome. These were exciting, erotic experiences.

While we continued to explore swinging, our entourage was amazingly growing. We found more people in Kansas City, interested in, or already experienced with, swinging, including some well-known faces and names. In fact, it reached the point that we decided to have our own swing, which actually became the first of a bunch.

I lived in a large home, with two black toy poodles, in an upscale South Kansas City, Missouri, neighborhood, when we first decided to entertain a group. John and I invited over a few friends, who expressed a desire to participate in this kind of party. We served cocktails and plenty of food. There was a fire in the fireplace and hot music playing. It was in the dead of winter and snow was falling, so we were careful to make sure the house was warm enough.

We had invited about six or seven couples, including people from all walks of life, businessmen, an officer of the Jaycees, a clothing buyer for a major department store chain, someone in the liquor business, a lawyer, a secretary, a nurse, among others.

Since I had a pool table, we played strip pool, as an icebreaker. It was a perfect way to start the party action. As it ended up, the party was a hit. Everyone had a great time and found it fulfilling.

Actually, there was one tiny hitch that came to our attention at the end of the party. It involved a married guest, who showed up with a girlfriend. When they were preparing to leave, a euphemism for getting dressed, the man discovered much to his shock, that his underwear had literally been shredded! His shorts were in thin, quarter inch strips, lots of thin strips. Remember my poodles?

My poodles, who had never torn a piece of clothing in their lives, and never did again, evidently felt compelled to do the unusual that night. Something about his shorts caused them to turn his shorts into confetti. I always wondered how he explained his disappearing underwear when he got home.

Following our first party, we continued on with our adventures. Through one of our guests that night, we were introduced to several more couples. Ultimately, we became close friends with some of these people. We spent many a lost weekend with them, over a period of time. In fact, it was during this period that I created my oral-sex singing, for which later I became so well known.

John and I still liked to go down the untrodden path, though, and see where it would take us. One night, at the Apartment Lounge, in Kansas City, we ran into a sexy, long golden-haired, blue-eyed stud, with whom I was acquainted. He had just returned from living in California, and could have easily been the surfers' poster child. The stud immediately began telling us about his partying life on the West Coast. Others joined in listening to the tales.

Finally, it was suggested that we move the group to a more personal setting, at a Country Club, which was across state line, in Overland Park, Kansas. Much to my astonishment, the lovely clubhouse itself became the heart of the swing. It was after hours, and one of our party people had full access to the club. It was one of the more amazing places I had ever seen group sex take place, especially in my hometown area. However, I was in for more surprises!

John loved to play jokes on people. I was no exception. One night we, with another couple, attended a lovely dinner dance at one of the hotels across from Arrowhead Stadium. He had told me it was involved with his business. It was a very dressy affair, and there were hundreds of people attending. People were incredibly friendly, and beautifully dressed. Most of them were actually very good-looking, as well.

As the evening continued, I finally realized we were at a dinner-dance of a swingers' organization, P.A.J.K., (pronounced payjack), visiting from St. Louis, Missouri. I figured it out when they had the drawing for the room keys as their means of getting the ball rolling. To say I was blown away, would be putting it mildly. We were surrounded by several hundred mostly married couples of various ages, all of whom were Midwestern swingers. Also, as I discovered, the night.

The first time, John and I walked those floors I know my mouth was hanging open, not for any other reason other than my total surprise. I felt like **Alice in Wonderland.** To see hundreds of couples cavorting naked in groups, or one-on-one, with the doors to their rooms open, all the way up and down the halls, was an unbelievable sight, especially in Kansas City, Missouri.

John and I met some great people in P.A.J.K., so we attended their next function in St Louis. We, also, met a dynamite couple, who had their own swings occasionally in their home in a wealthy St. Louis suburb. When it was possible to get away from Kansas City, we loved going to their parties.

P.A.J.K. generally had a function about once a month. Since we had joined, we received their monthly newsletter, which was fairly typical of any organization's newsletter.

A few short years later, after John and I had parted ways, romantically, (although we remained close friends), I became an erotic film star. During that time in my life, I saw the world of swinging on both coasts, as well as in the heartland.

There were other swinging and threesome incidents in my life, but it wasn't until I became well known as an erotic film and stage star, and was writing for men's magazines, did I realize that swinging had entered the world of big business.

Continued on page 86

Afternoon Delight

One of the advantages of fantasy phone sex is that callers can enjoy by means of a fantasy what they might be extremely hesitant to do in real life. While this is certainly not always the case, sometimes the phone sex fantasy fulfills that desire as far as the caller really wants to go with it.

One early summer evening, I received such a call from Wally, of Green Bay, Wisconsin, who claimed to be a single, dark-haired, average-looking guy. Wally, an executive with a manufacturing company, told me he was attracted to women's faces, first. He was especially turned on by making eye contact with a woman whose face attracted him. If he liked a woman's face, her body shape and size did not particularly matter, as far as he was concerned. Wally had seen one of my movies where I happened to look into the camera several times, and Wally felt I was looking straight at him. In his mind, we had made eye contact. Plus, my face turned him on. So, he was excited when he discovered an ad that stated he could talk to me through Personal Services Club.

Wally told me his fantasies always involved

surprises. He loved to give surprises and to receive them. That was where he wanted to go with his fantasy on this night. Before Wally had called, he had already worked out the fantasy's details, too.

Wally's phone sex fantasy begins with having me living with him. In his fantasy he goes to work one Monday, and decides it's a day for a surprise. He leaves his office at noon to come home and surprise me with his early arrival. He plans on making love to me when he gets there.

However, Wally finds his own surprise when he walks in. I am in the bedroom, but I am not alone. There's a good-looking couple, Bart and Molly, with me, and we are steaming up the room. I am sucking Bart, and Molly is going down on me, at the same time.

After recovering from the pleasant shock of what he discovers, Wally rips off his clothes and joins us. After giving me a quick kiss, he eats Molly's pussy. While he's doing that, Bart and I fuck doggie style. Molly begins sucking Wally. Meanwhile, Wally watches Bart cum inside me while we are fucking.

Next, while Bart relaxes, I take over sucking Wally. Then, Molly and I suck Wally together. Bart watches the action. Molly rims Wally while I continue sucking him. He is so turned on that he pulls me over, lays me on my back, and fucks me deep with my legs wrapped around his neck. Molly is massaging and licking his butt, too, while we are fucking. Wally is so boiling hot he quickly orgasms.

After Wally came, he told me he did not think he would ever have the nerve to participate in a foursome, but he loved the idea and the fantasy. He also said he would love to be married to a woman like me. He added that if his spouse ever arranged something like a group sex activity as a surprise, then, maybe he could possibly do it. He wanted it, but he was also afraid of it. I understood.

Before we hung up, Wally laughingly told me he was going to come up with more surprises for our next call. As time progressed, all Wally's calls to me contained a surprise theme, and usually some form of group sex.

Occasionally, I even got to surprise Wally, which he loved.

I figured Wally would never fulfill his group sex fantasy, but I knew he had a lot of fun fantasizing about it, and surprises were something he could fulfill any time he wished.

* * * *

Rich's Heat Trigger

A just turned twenty-seven-year-old from Dallas, Texas, named Rich, called one evening, saying he was in a very sexual mood. Rich, as it turned out, had been watching some erotic films at home that evening, and had gotten to thinking about his own fantasies. He mentioned his fantasy level had expanded, too, from previously watching my movies.

Rich said his wife was a nurse, who worked long hours. Unfortunately, their hours conflicted, so they rarely saw each other. This made it hard on their lovemaking, or it caused a lack of lovemaking. He said they had been having sex problems on the rare occasions they made love. He was having trouble having an orgasm with his wife, and rarely did.

Working on computer programs for an automobile manufacturer was Rich's career. He said that took a lot of thinking and frustration, but he enjoyed it just the same. Rich said he felt fantastic when things came together in his job.

At last, Rich turned to his fantasies and turn ons. Rich told me that he loved to fuck, and his favorite position was with the girl on top. He was crazy about going down on women. Also, Rich absolutely loved women's breasts, especially their nipples. He didn't care about the sizes or shapes of breasts, but was crazy about the nipples most of all. He especially was thrilled about hard, erect nipples, and he loved to suck them.

While Rich was telling me all these things, it was obvious he was getting hot. However, there was more to come. His ultimate turn on was watching what he called "girl – girl scenes." He explained that he found watching two women lick each other's nipples, and making them hard and erect, was the top heat trigger for him!

line was smoking. It was apparent the time had come for his fantasy phone sex.

Rich wants a three-some with me and my good friend, and fellow erotic actress, Samantha Fox. He starts with the three of us naked in his king-sized bed. He watches Samantha and I tongue-kiss. Then, Samantha licks my nipples and gets them erect. He requests that we lie down next to each other, in his fantasy, and we play with each other's breasts, while he watches. He takes turns going down on each of us. Rich starts with Samantha, then, goes to me. Meanwhile, Samantha and I take turns sucking each other's tits. Then, he desires to fuck us. He lies back, and Samantha sits on him, and he reaches up and pulls and pinches her nipples while he fucks her. Meanwhile, he is also fingering me, and sucking my breasts. Then, Rich wants to fuck me in the same position. While we are doing that, Samantha licks his testicles, which drives him wild. Finally, he wishes for her to suck my breasts, while I am riding him. As she is sucking my hard nipples, it becomes too much for Rich, and he has what sounds like a huge orgasm!

Rich had some other details he wanted in his three-some fantasy, but he came so hard that we decided he would have to save them for another time. In fact, before we hung up, Rich shared one more fantasy that he fully intended to fulfill someday. He wanted to take a champagne bath with a lover.

I liked talking to Rich. He was a nice, warm, friendly guy. I looked forward to talking with him again. In fact, I ended up talking to him a great deal, over the years.

* * * *

Horny KC Fireman

Johnny, a fireman from Kansas City, Missouri, had horny hormones. He told me he worked long shifts, and ended up with a lot of time on his hands. He said looking at men's magazines and watching erotic movies got old after awhile and he would want the real thing. Since having a woman in the flesh wasn't feasible at that time, he wanted the next best thing, talking dirty on the phone, with a sexy woman. Johnny called me because he had seen my stage shows, and watched some of my movies in Kansas City. He desired a woman to whom he could somehow relate. He wanted to know what she looked like and what she could do. After all, Johnny was from the Show Me state.

Watching two gorgeous women getting it

on with each other is Johnny's top fantasy. Since he had previously seen Outlaw Ladies, Johnny is enamored with a great scene between Samantha Fox, Joey Silvera, and me. He tells me all the things he likes about this sizzling scene. It is apparent he's enjoying himself while talking about it.

Johnny, then, requests I create a fantasy between Samantha and me, doing girl-girl sex, He wants it to occur when she and I were in Kansas City for the premiere of Outlaw Ladies. One of the key ingredients for his fantasy is that Samantha and I use what is known as a double-headed dildo on each other. He, also, wants to be present to watch.

When he finds himself completely turned on, Johnny comes over to me, in his fantasy, and has me suck him, until he gets off, which is instantly. Johnny is not through, however. After getting off, he talks about liking to watch women on their hands and knees, and abruptly decides he wants more. This time, he still wants me with Samantha, but on my hands and knees, and he comes up behind me while she and I are continuing with girl-girl activities, and he finishes fulfilling his fantasy by having anal sex with me. In an extremely quick fashion, Johnny is successful in getting off a second time.

Johnny was somewhat unusual in that he was able to have two orgasms so quickly and so close together. However, with variations, his fantasies of women with women were fairly common. Johnny always wanted threesomes in his fantasy phone calls, and usually had two orgasms. He was definitely a hot and horny fireman!

Continued from page 78

When I was with **Cheri** magazine, **Cheri** magazine's senior editor and my good friend, the late Peter Wolff, and I used to often check out the scene at Plato's Retreat for the publication. People joined Plato's Retreat, as a club, and then paid a heavy cover charge. The place was popular, and as it became more of an "in" spot in Manhattan, it even had to move to larger quarters. There were multiple rooms for multiple sexual purposes available. Peter, like any good editor of men's magazines, was a great voyeur, and he was always quick to point out anything interesting that was happening. We could sit in what was the main room and have cocktails, some food, and be entertained by watching naked swimmers doing all kinds of erotic acrobats in the indoor pool, or we could look through an all glass wall into a huge softly-lit room, filled with wall-to-wall mattresses, and always filled with naked people enjoying themselves.

There was another area, down a long hallway, that

had small rooms on each side, with a kind of mini-caves look. These were rooms without doors where two, three, or perhaps four could go for more intimate sex, but the rooms were too small for any more than that. Usually, there were only two or three people in them. Of course, people could also have some sexual activity in the main room, too. There were other playrooms there, as well, over the years. It was definitely a hot hangout. It was hot enough that over time I even managed to squeeze in a couple of songs at Plato's, enjoying my own exploits.

Rock stars, television, and film actors and actresses could sometimes be seen in there. I frequently saw a famous plastic surgeon hanging out. Professional athletes were observed having cocktails and enjoying the action. Plato's Retreat was one of the places to go to literally see what was happening on the sex scene in New York, and, at the same time, it was making its mark in the history of swinging.

There was one occasion when Plato's Retreat was left behind, and Peter and I, with some other **Cheri** staffers, did check out a major swing held in a Manhattan converted loft. It was by invitation only and it cost money to attend. We found it filled with at least 250 plus naked bodies when we arrived. After chatting with a lot of the undressed bunch, it was apparent the majority were professional people. I especially enjoyed a sexy gynecologist, no less!

Continued on page 95

Orgy in Ontario

Dudley, from Ontario, Canada, called one evening, ready to party. He told me he was a geologist for oil companies, who had had a tough day and now he wanted a wild night! Dudley said he could never do his fantasies in real life because it would cause him great embarrassment, and could damage his career, among other reasons.

Abruptly, Dudley changed the subject and began talking about the longitudes and latitudes of Ontario, and Northern California. In fact, he continued talked about geology, in general, for a short time.

Just as suddenly, Dudley was back on the subject of sex. He said he was ready to discuss his fantasy with me. He apologetically told me it was probably a little extreme, but it was what he wanted.

In his phone fantasy, Dudley desires for me to accompany him to a party. We get to the party and discover it's an orgy. We wander around and watch people having group sex. It looks like an

adult playground with all the hot action. There is heavy rock playing in the background.

Then, we open a door to an oversized bedroom, where we find six guys and a couple of women. They are all in one big pile getting it on. Dudley is very turned on by now. He starts kissing and groping me. One of the six guys comes over and decides to join in. The hunk undresses me and begins sucking my breasts. He tells Dudley to get naked. Dudley takes off his clothes and is rubbing himself against me. The naked stud grabs Dudley's cock and strokes it. He offers his own to Dudley. Dudley gets on his knees and sucks the guy. While he's doing that, the guy backs up and sits on the bed, and motions for me to lie on the bed next to him. He eats me. All the while, Dudley is sucking him.

Everyone in the room is paying attention to us, now. The other guys join us. The naked girls just sit down on the floor and watch the action. I have a guy in my mouth, another is playing with my breasts. The fourth fellow goes down on Dudley. The other two stand there stroking themselves, watching, and waiting.

Meanwhile, Dudley unexpectedly desires to fuck me. He comes up to the bed, where I am lying on my back, and enters me. While he is doing that, one of the guys, a good-looking blond, reaches down and plays with Dudley's testicles. He squeezes Dudley's buttocks, and plays with his anal area. Dudley continues fucking me through all this.

Now, the blond has anal sex with Dudley while he is still in me. With the blond's initial thrust, Dudley definitely gets off from being the middle of a sandwich. He climaxes hard and loud. His phone fantasy is a success.

After the fantasy was fulfilled, Dudley thanked me for allowing him to have his hot fantasy. He told me I was very nice and very sexy. He wished he could meet me sometime, but knew that probably wouldn't happen. However, he said he would be calling again.

* * * *

Emmitt's Cruel Punishment

An intriguing man, named Emmitt, called one night from the San Diego area. He told me his girlfriend was on "probation" with him, because of some embarrassing incident. So, as part of her punishment, he wasn't having sex with her for at least a couple of weeks. My immediate thought was that he was a sexist, although I did not say anything. However, as he spoke more on the subject, I could see how he was responding to both hurt and embarrassment caused by the girlfriend.

Emmitt described himself as a great-looking, really dark African-American, with black hair and brown eyes, 6 feet tall, and 175 pounds. He claimed he looked like a leaner Billy Dee Williams, although he was a business executive, not an actor. Throughout the call, Emmitt frequently mentioned his good looks. Emmitt, also, casually threw in that he was built like a "stud star" in sexual areas, too.

Wine, (preferably Chablis), Scotch, and Bourbon were all favorites of Emmitt, as he explained he wasn't fussy about his cocktails when he was kicking back, and getting mellow with a woman. In addition to virtually any cocktail, Emmitt enjoyed George Benson music medleys when he was making love.

Besides the cocktails and music, Emmitt told me what made his lovemaking sessions complete, (with a sexy woman, of course), doing it in his waterbed. There were mirrors on the ceiling, directly above the bed, he added.

At this point, Emmitt decided to talk about me, telling me on a scale of one to ten I was a "number 10 man killer." While he was commenting on me, I could hear his George Benson music in the background. Emmitt continued telling me how horny I made him, and how he just couldn't get enough sex to fill his appetite.

Finally, Emmitt was ready for the sexy part of his phone call.

We are in his bedroom and we are naked. He

grabs me and throws me on the waterbed. Then, Emmitt touches me, running his dark hands all over my body, caressing me everywhere. After that, he kisses me all the places he has touched me with his hands, which includes my entire body. He sucks my breasts and he licks my pussy, as well. Then, he comes up and straddles my chest, while I am lying on my back. He has me suck him, in this position.

Now, Emmitt is ready to fuck. He starts fucking me by simply moving down my body, and raising my spread legs straight up in the air. Then, he fucks me with us lying on our sides, facing each other. After that, he lays back and has me on top. Finally, I get on all fours, and we fuck, in the phone fantasy, doggie style. This is the position we are in when Emmitt has a dynamite orgasm.

Emmitt was an extremely hot and horny man, who was absolutely crazy about sex. He also mentioned he loved swinging, and was curious about what it would take to join one of the premiere swingers' clubs in America, the A-Frame, in the Hollywood area.

While he was still on the phone he mentioned a desire to get into porn, too. He felt he had an insatiable appetite for sex, yet, at the same time, great control. Emmitt figured that would help him handle his desires.

I thought Emmitt came across as a highly erotic guy. He also seemed sexually sophisticated. I wished him well in his real pursuit of his sexual dreams.

* * * *

Stressed Air Controller

Early one midweek evening, I received a call from Arnold, a Canadian, from Toronto. Arnold described himself as being about 6 feet tall and having brown eyes and dark brown curly hair. He said he was single, but didn't particularly enjoy the singles' bar scene anymore. Arnold's career was highly stressful as he was an air-traffic controller. So, when he felt uptight or horny, he would call for a sexy phone fantasy.

Arnold's calls to Personal Services always had the same basic theme with some variations. Sometimes, he desired to be a participant and other times he only wanted to watch. He was specifically interested in girl-girl experiences.

The night Arnold called me, he told me he had seen several of my movies, and he wanted details on any girl-girl scenes in them. Then, he wanted to talk about a scene from one of my movies, **Outlaw Ladies**, which he really liked, involving Samantha Fox, (actor) Joey Silvera, and me. After discussing it, Arnold was ready for his phone sex fantasy.

Arnold is scorching hot, so he immediately

gets into the threesome he desires. The threesome includes him, Samantha, and me. Initially, in the fantasy, Arnold has Samantha sit on his face, while he licks her pussy. At the same time, he requests I "chew on his cock," which were his words for sucking his cock. After doing those things he has Samantha turn around while he's still eating her, so she is facing me. Now, he wishes for me to sit on his cock, facing Samantha. Then, Arnold desires for Samantha and me to French kiss, plus, play with each other's breasts while I'm riding him, and he's eating her. I lean slightly back and Samantha leans forward to suck my breasts, too. This final act in the fantasy causes Arnold to shoot his cum in me.

Since Arnold was out of breath after his hard orgasm, he did not have a whole lot to say. He did tell me how much he enjoyed his fantasy and that he would get a good night's sleep. Arnold said for me to expect to hear from him again.

Arnold seemed like a nice fellow, with a tough, but important job. I was pleased I could help him relax, and I knew his phone sex fantasy with me was better than any sleeping pill. I was sure his next call would be a pleasant one.

After being in New York for a while, it was always nice to go home for a visit to Kansas City, Missouri. Besides, since I wrote a column about activities going on in that area of the country, I needed to sometimes check things out on a personal level. However, I figured there were not any more surprises in store for me, on the swinging safari, especially in Kansas City. I was wrong!

When I arrived in K.C., some friends met me at the airport with new tales of swinging excitement. They told me a swingers' organization (club) had started in Kansas City. I found it a little hard to believe, but they were insistent it had happened. One of my friends, an investigator in the prosecutor's office, said he knew where the club's founders, a married couple, frequently had cocktails. I decided if this Spirit of '76, the name of the swinger's organization, actually existed, it would make good material for my column. So, he and I headed out south to that Kansas City nightclub before I even unpacked.

There we met the founders of the Spirit of '76. They were nice people who were thrilled with the idea of being written about in a national magazine. They had a function coming up soon and invited me, and any friends I desired to bring with me, as their guests. I decided I had to see what these people had created, so I agreed to come.

My friend, the investigator, who was strictly a friend, asked me to please take him along to the affair, which was going to be held in a very nice, multi-storied, Hickman Mills motel. He figured, rightly, he could give me a little protection, if needed, from overly exuberant fans.

When we arrived at the party we discovered there were over 200 couples present. Their dance was fun, rowdy, and casual. Finally, as the evening progressed, people began gravitating toward the rooms. The club had reserved all the rooms on three floors, so, we decided to roam around the reserved floors, and see if there was any action.

I had seen a lot of sexual activities in the swinging world, but never in my wildest dreams did I ever expect to see well over 400 local, (unlike P.A.J.K. where most of the party goers were from out-of-town), naked people, running around, and participating in various forms of sex in a suburban motel in my hometown, Kansas City!

As we strolled down the halls, we saw a number of people actually doing sexual deeds in the halls. All room doors were open, and some of the nude men or women stood at the doors alluringly calling out to us like hucksters in San Francisco's North Beach, or on Bourbon Street in New Orleans, peddling their rooms' sexual happenings. However, we resisted the temptations, and my friend and I continued our amazing walk down the halls of the three floors. Sometimes, we would stop and go into a room to observe the events though, totally astonished by our fellow Kansas Citians.

When we did go into rooms, we would see anywhere from about four to twenty people in every possible sexual position. In most cases they were doing group activities. Only rarely did we see a couple enjoying each other alone.

I talked with as many of the local swingers as possible, and discovered that their ages ranged from 21 through 78, and all in-between ages. Their ages may have been extremely different, but their enthusiasm and delight in their swinging ways was about the same. Also, over 90 percent of the people were participating with their spouses. The others were mostly with longtime lovers. Everybody was especially friendly, too.

Afterward, my investigator friend told me he loved the experience, and asked if we could go again. Since the founders gave me an honorary membership, and I agreed to at least occasionally make a personal appearance, when home, I decided to take him another time. Besides, I was curious if Spirit of '76 could sustain the numbers that we saw there. They were successful.

Continued on page 103

Swinging Fascination

It was always nice to hear from Johnny, a repeat caller and fan, from Omaha, Nebraska. Johnny owned an insurance brokerage firm there, and enjoyed getting away from the business pressures, to call me, once or twice a month. He always liked to chat about different things relating to the world of erotica, or about different aspects of my life or career. On rare occasions, Johnny wanted to do more than chat, but usually chatting was what he wished to do.

On those very rare occasions, when Johnny was into doing more, his desires always involved oral sex and fucking. However, even on those calls, the sex was extremely brief, and he would continue talking about other matters, afterward.

This call, Johnny casually asked how a pattern photography project, in which I was involved, was coming along. Also, he wanted to talk about my and Samantha Fox's photo in **X-Rated Stars**
that was on the stands, at the time.

The subject that most interested Johnny this particular night, though, was swinging. Johnny had read a couple of articles I had written on swinging, and he had lots of questions. He began with the East Coast and worked his way to the Midwest.

Johnny wanted me to tell him about Plato's Retreat, in New York City, which had been the most famous swingers' club in America. I attempted to fill him in with all the intimate details about this hedonistic, pleasure palace.

Then, Johnny mentioned two well-known, private swingers' clubs in the Midwest, Spirit of '76 and P.A.J.K. (founders first name initial's). Spirit of '76 originated in Kansas City, Missouri, and P.A.J.K.'s hometown was St. Louis. Since I personally had attended dances and affairs of both these clubs, I was able to answer most of his questions. Johnny was so intrigued by these midwestern clubs, I later wondered if he would try to join either of them. If he did try, he was going to need a partner of the opposite sex to join with him. Like virtually all private swingers' clubs, memberships were only available to couples.

When Johnny was saturated with information and anecdotes about these swingers' clubs, the call ended. I enjoyed chatting with him, as usual, and I knew he was happy that I increased his knowledge on things that fascinated him. I did not have any doubts I would hear from him, again, soon.

* * * *

Xmas After-Party

When I was doing fantasy phone sex, I would get all kinds of calls from all kinds of people with an infinite variety of fantasies. One of my calls that was a little bit different was from Duke, in Boston. Duke, a city theatrical actor, said he was thirty-five-years-old, single, 5 feet 8 inches tall, and weighed 165 pounds.

Duke began telling me about his fantasy almost immediately. It was somewhat complicated, so he wanted me to have a chance to digest it for a minute. As he explained it, I felt I understood what he meant.

His fantasy begins with us coming home from a festive Christmas party. While we are at the party, we meet a couple, both about nineteen-years-old, named John and Lisa. After several cocktails, we invite them over to the house to join us in some intimate fun.

When we get to the house, he has only the two of us undress and put on some very sexy, silky lingerie. We both put on stockings, garter belts and peignoirs. He, also, lays out similar outfits for the young man and woman, who are joining us.

After the couple arrives, Duke tells the couple to change their clothes. They gladly comply. Further, he makes it known to them he would like them to be obedient to our sexual orders. The couple is very turned on and immediately agrees to his wishes.

In the phone fantasy, Duke wants Lisa to go down on both of us; first, on me. He wants John to suck my breasts, at the same time. Everybody is to leave on the lingerie, he says. After Lisa eats me for a while, he wants her to suck him. Then, he wants both of us to suck him, at the same time. He desires watching John fucking me, at this point, while Lisa continues sucking him. Now, he wants to eat my pussy and, then, Lisa's. Following that, he fucks both Lisa and me. He watches me suck John, and he is very excited. He requests John go down on him, and while that is occurring, Duke finally cums.

Afterward, Duke made a point of telling me that he would never do anything like his fantasy in his real life, but, that, in actuality, he had problems getting off, sometimes. So, he had discovered that his complex fantasies usually resolved that for him. He said the phone fantasies helped later when he made love with his lady friend.

* * * *

Wild Fantasies

A twenty-four-year-old, single AT&T customer manager, from Atlanta, named Lou, called one evening, telling me how he loved "all kinds of wild sex." Well, I had learned words like that could go in any direction, so I waited to hear more before determining what Lou wanted to do. Come to find out, Lou had a variety of fantasies. His fantasies ran the course from pretty basic sex involving fucking and oral sex, to a submissive fantasy, and, finally, to learning to suck another man's cock. That evening, he wanted a couple of those combined.

Lou desires to start out by going down on me. Then, he wants to fuck me in the so-called missionary position. Finally, Lou wants to cum on my breasts. Following his orgasm, Lou expresses the desire to lick his cum off my breasts, which he, then, does.

Lou still wants more from his fantasies. He requests I now include a certain male actor from one of my movies. This is the person on whom he wishes me to teach him oral sex. So, I now give Lou lessons in the art of cocksucking, which he tells me he has never done.

Then, Lou requests that the fantasy, erotic film actor come on my breasts, just as he had earlier. At that point, Lou proceeds to lick this actor's cum off my breasts. Lou is fulfilled, at last.

One of the advantages of phone sex was the callers could safely test out some of their fantasies, without taking chances or endangering themselves. Lou had fantasies, including his submissive fantasy, that, perhaps, he would not want to do in reality because of the potential problems that could possibly go with actually doing them. Fantasy phone sex gave him an outlet to enjoy himself without taking the risks.

Continued from page 97

As my career continued, I began spending more time on the West Coast, where I figured everything was taking place, anyway. So, I did not give any thought to any more swinging surprises.

I happened to be in Los Angeles with an actor friend of mine, on business, when some friends contacted me, asking if I could get them into a certain prestigious swingers' club. They had called the club and had not gotten anywhere when inquiring about joining. I agreed to look into it.

I anonymously called the club inquiring about membership, and also got the runaround. Then, I called back and immediately identified myself. This time, I was given the president of the club, who invited me, with my actor friend, to the club, and, furthermore, said there wouldn't be any charges for us. In fact, he gave me a free membership on the spot, which also included a monthly publication. Now, I was going to be receiving three swingers' publications a month!

I still hadn't resolved my friends' problem. So, I asked the head of the club why it was such a hassle for people to get memberships in this club. Well, his answer was as intriguing as anything else I had ever heard or seen in the swinging jungle. He informed me it was the beautiful people's swingers' club. Most people had to fill out a questionnaire and enclose their photographs, to even be considered for membership. Then, if a person made it that far, that person had to be personally met by management the first time there to see if he or she looked like the picture and matched the information supplied. He further told me they turned down more applications than they accepted. The questions included such things as height, weight, color of eyes, hair, marital status, field, etc. He said they wanted to know about scars, or anything that could mar a member's looks, in their opinion. This time I was shocked. My friends had their hearts set on this place, so I continued to try and get them in without all this nonsense.

The president finally agreed they could come, and if they met the club's standards they could, then, do the paperwork. Don, my actor friend, and I agreed to go with them their first time.

The club was in a huge, gorgeous multi-million dollar home, high up in the Hollywood Hills. This was swingers' big business, West Coast style. The home's interior had been gutted and rebuilt strictly for the purpose of swinging. The owners did not live on the premises, but lived in homes nearby.

We watched everyone in line in front of us be checked on a list, and, then, pay money. We were on a very short, separate list and were welcomed in without a dime changing hands.

The first thing I noticed was the house was elegant, yet practical, for constant crowds and sex. The second thing I noticed was the dancing. I had never seen so many good-looking, naked people dancing at one time. Most people were completely undressed, although some were still wearing a few little pieces of lingerie or undies. Actually, there were two rooms for dancing.

Several bars were located in the house, serving drinks. There were even nearly naked waitresses. Two large halls were lined with tiny rooms, similar to Plato's Retreat, except these had curtains covering the openings, and they were just large enough to hold mattresses. There were about forty of these tiny rooms. On the other side of the house, overlooking Hollywood, there were special bedrooms, with king-sized beds for special people to enjoy. Smaller rooms and alcoves were attached to these rooms for private moments. The club, of course, had the prerequisite giant everybody-naked-in-a-pile room. It was packed!!! Outside, overlooking the city we were greeted by two huge pool-sized hot tubs.

Don and I decided to try out the hot tubs. From there, we could look right and get a beautiful view of the city, and if we looked left, we could enjoy the view of the beautiful people sexually cavorting inside the house. The house was constructed deliberately so that most of it was a voyeur's dream. Except for the curtained rooms and the Special VIP rooms, everybody could see most of the action.

The club president didn't lie. Both the men and women were all beautiful, including my friends, who passed the beauty test. The place was jumping. Don and I estimated there were about 600 people there. While the sex was essentially the same as other swingers' clubs, the atmosphere was very "California."

I did visit the beautiful people's club a few more times, at later dates, with a cinematographer, who I was seeing. We had fun, although I was never really comfortable with the club's way of determining membership. I always wondered how many sharp people got rejected for superficial reasons.

Continued on page 114

Hollywood Threesome

An interesting call came from a Hollywood actor, one fall evening. He was a new caller who had become intrigued by me after seeing my movies. So, he decided to give me a call when he saw the opportunity existed.

The actor, named Lee, discussed my movies and his films. He told me all the things I did that turned him on in my movies. Also, he told me he was a breast man and loved sexy lingerie on women.

Then, Lee surprised me by putting me on a speakerphone and telling me he wasn't alone. At that point, a sultry-voiced female said hello to me. Lee's girlfriend, Heidi, was there with him, and wanted to participate in the call. Lee loved the idea!

Our conversation turned to swinging. Lee and Heidi told me they belonged to several swingers' clubs. Their favorite one was a large membership club, located in Orange County. Their second favorite was a smaller one, in the Hollywood area. Heidi mentioned that they loved threesomes, as well.

Finally, Lee tells me what he and Heidi want for their fantasy. Initially, he wants me to do a slow, sensual striptease, but leave on my black, satin garter belt and long, sheer, black stockings. Following that, Lee wishes for me to lick his entire body and go down on him, while Heidi watches us.

Then, Lee and Heidi want me to teach her some special oral sex techniques, including vibrations, among others. So, in the phone fantasy, I explain, demonstrate, and tell her how to suck him. She really does this to him as I teach her.

Lee decides he wants to suck and play with my breasts while Heidi is sucking him, according to my previous instructions. He gets really turned on and he now verbalizes how he would go down on me. Heidi continues to suck him.

As Lee gets closer to orgasm, he asks me to

go down on him with Heidi. Heidi is an excellent student. We suck him together, licking and sucking his testicles, as well. Lee suddenly has a hard orgasm with both of us going down on him, at the same time. In reality, he comes that hard, orally, with Heidi. She tells me how much she enjoyed it, while Lee is still trying to catch his breath. She thanks me for adding so much to their love games.

Lee and Heidi were one very hot, enthusiastic couple. They invited me to join them on his yacht, for a vacation, sometime. I figured that would be one wild time, but I passed on it. However, I did enjoy this couple with their positive, sexy, upbeat, sensual attitudes. They were lots of fun and I hoped to hear from them again.

* * * *

Naughty Nicole

Early one spring morning, I received a call from Neil, of Birmingham, Alabama. Neil, who was a civil servant for the state of Alabama, had previously seen three of my movies. He liked me in them, and when the opportunity presented itself, he decided to call me. Neil said he was very slender, standing 6 feet tall, but only weighing 140 pounds. He had black hair and true blue eyes, he added.

Neil told me he was married to Nicole, who he proudly described as 5 feet 2 inches tall, with semi-long brown hair, big brown eyes, and a soft, pretty face. She also had a slender waist, and 34-inch, C-Cup tits. I thought it was interesting that Neil described his wife in such detail, and I wondered where all this was going.

Next, Neil talked about a black man, with whom he worked. He said the black fellow, Wilbur, had been a close friend of his for about six years. Wilbur was a good-looking guy, who stood 6 feet 3 inches tall, and weighed 200 pounds. Neil was impressed with Wilbur's fantastic body, and charming personality. As for me, I was getting dizzy from all the weights and heights.

Finally, he began bringing the players together.

For about a year, Neil had been fantasizing about his wife, Nicole, having a sexual affair with Wilbur. He said he had thought of it many times while making love with his wife, and he had also masturbated to the idea, frequently. However, he had never told anyone about his fantasy, before me.

Then, the bombshell dropped on his life. He was devastated when he had recently found out his good friend, Wilbur, had actually been regularly fucking his wife for several months. Additionally, Nicole had been screwing Wilbur's roommate, as well. Sometimes, Nicole fucked them together, and, other times, separately. Furthermore, he found out, at the same time, that Wilbur had a thick, 9-inch cock, which, in his mind, added insult to injury, because he now felt inadequate with his 5-inch cock.

Now, Neil's life was all upside down. He and Wilbur were hardly speaking to each other. His marriage was on the rocks, and he knew the sexual affair had not ended between Wilbur and Nicole.

Neil became so emotional telling me his story I figured that all he wanted to do was share it with me, and see if that helped him move on. I was wrong. Neil was more complicated than that.

At this time, Neil requested the fulfillment of his unusual phone sex fantasy, which did not include either of us in it. Instead, I was to create a third person scenario, which only included Wilbur and Nicole. He wanted me to tell a detailed story where Nicole and Wilbur had great sex together. He was not to be mentioned in the story, he reminded me, again, not even by inference. Neil even outlined what he wanted covered in the scenario.

He wants Wilbur and Nicole at a club drinking and dancing. Afterward, they go to her and Neil's home together. Neil is very specific about that. Wilbur makes out with Nicole, and she hotly responds. They French kiss; they do all the little foreplay tricks. Wilbur plays with her breasts through her silk blouse. He puts her hand on his crotch. Neil asks me to describe how Wilbur's big cock grows hard under her hand, in his pants.

Then, Wilbur unzips his pants and pulls out his cock, and Nicole goes down on him. Wilbur undresses Nicole, and takes her into Neil's and her bedroom. Nicole sits on the side of the bed with Wilbur standing in front of her. She sucks him, and she loves it. He pushes her down and licks her pussy. She cums hard. Wilbur gets on her and pounds her with his strong fucking, while her legs are wrapped around him tight. She squirms and screams, and gets off again. Now, Wilbur cums in Nicole.

As my storytelling progresses, I hear Neil breathing harder and harder. When Wilbur cums, Neil suddenly yells out and cums, too, virtually at the same time.

After Neil's orgasm, he talked about how much the tale turned him on, and how he loved seeing the contrast of Nicole's pale white body against Wilbur's charcoal black body. At the same time, he again mentioned how hurt he was by her and Wilbur's actions. Neil said he was confused by his mixed feelings. He was depressed a lot, he said, but he felt better finally baring his heart and emotions to someone.

I found Neil's call intriguing. The man was obviously suffering, but used the source of his suffering to backtrack to his original personal fantasy, (and as it turned out, reality), and actually get off on it. I wondered if there wasn't a little bit of masochism in him. Regardless, he seemed like a very nice guy, and I was somewhat fascinated by his complexity. I was curious where his ironic tale was going to lead, too. So, when Neil asked me if he could please call me, again, because he felt so comfortable talking to me, I definitely said yes. As future calls with Neil showed, there were still all kinds of surprises ahead, and I was his number one audience.

* * * *

Minnesota Swingers

I heard from Gary, of St. Paul, Minnesota, on a blustery, Midwest, March evening. Gary told me he was single, 5 feet 11 inches, 185-pounds, had blond hair and blue eyes. He said he was an Investment Broker, who was turned on by beautiful, sexy women. Gary, also, claimed he was a Minnesota swinger, who belonged to local swing clubs.

I was intrigued by this statement because I had had a previous caller from the greater Minneapolis area, who, also, belonged to the same swingers' clubs! However, I did not tell Gary about the other caller because that would have been unethical, in my opinion.

Gary talked quite a bit about two swingers' clubs, Playhouse Swing Club and The Silver Chain. He said he had spent a lot of time swinging at the Playhouse, but since he had become a member of The Silver Chain, (which he described as a very exclusive club); he preferred his swinging there. He liked their ambiance and party people better. He made it clear, though, there was certainly nothing wrong with the Playhouse Swing Club.

Then, Gary changed directions by commenting how disappointed he was that I had never appeared at The Faust Theatre, in the Minneapolis area. He had seen a few of my movies and had hoped I would appear there. Gary had previously seen a couple of my good friends, Samantha Fox and Juliet Anderson, onstage at that theatre.

Finally, Gary came to the subject of his own erotic fantasy that he wanted in his call.

Gary has the two of us, already naked, in his bed. He begins by kissing my forehead and he slowly, sensuously moves down me, kissing me everywhere. Gary wants me to just lie there and enjoy, during this part. After kissing me on the lips he moves down to my breasts, which he kisses and sucks. He continues down my body to my inner thighs as he slightly spreads my legs. He continues moving his tongue and lips down my legs to my feet. Then, Gary travels back up my legs, gradually spreading them more apart. He gets to my upper inner thighs, and, this time, he continues kissing and licking me up to my pussy. When he gets to my pussy, he eats me. Then, Gary requests that we "69." So, he turns around, having me on the bottom. While we are "69ing," Gary has a great orgasm.

Gary sounded like he truly enjoyed himself when he got off. He told me he felt really great, and had a lot of fun talking with me. Also, he again expressed his desire for me to do a stage show at a theatre in Minneapolis. We finished the call with Gary telling me I would be hearing from him in the very near future.

Continued from page 106

John, my old boyfriend, and I began our safari into the sexual, swinging jungle, never dreaming where it would lead. Then, when I got into erotic films, I didn't realize that my adventures were going to continue. However, they did.

I learned a lot about other people and their sexuality, and even some more about my own sexuality during those swinging experiences. The golden age of swinging was a fascinating time, and I am glad I got to be involved in some of its history.

When I began doing fantasy phone sex calls, I quickly discovered that many callers' fantasies involved three or more people. With all the swinging to which I had been exposed, I found them to be generally easy and enjoyable calls. This particular chapter contained only a few calls detailing one of the most popular fantasies that my callers ever requested.

CHAPTER 4

DIFFERENT STROKES

When I began receiving calls through Personal Services Club, I soon discovered that a number of calls were of a different nature than what most people would expect. The club had somewhat intellectually prepared me for the eventuality of such calls, yet, I knew these kinds of calls were not my strong areas of expertise. I was, to some extent, unfamiliar, or a little inexperienced, with certain desires, on a personal level; however, I had occasionally run across a few people with really unique yearnings, in my private life or through my career. So, I was fully aware that there were these different kinds of desires for some people.

This is not to say I was totally in the dark in these fields, but they definitely were not my most knowledgeable areas.

To prepare for certain kinds of calls, I talked to people who were more familiar with the unusual interests, and I drew upon my writing experiences, and past research for a couple of magazines, as well. Plus, the young medical student, who was considered the resident female expert at Personal Services Club on such calls, was kind enough to give me a few pointers.

Perhaps, some of my greatest help and resourcefulness, for these kinds of calls, though, came from my previous research for a couple of stories I had written for magazines.

When I was with **Cheri** magazine I wrote a monthly column, as well as feature stories. Most of my column's pieces were true stories about real people from the heartland, running the gamut from covering Al Goldstein's trial, **Screw** magazine, for alleged obscenity in Wichita, Kansas, to Midwesterners' sexual activities. I also looked for the unusual or outrageous, occurring in the greater vicinity of my hometown, Kansas City, Missouri.

During one of my visits back home, I found out that a Kansas City acquaintance had successfully opened a B and D, and S and M business, on Main Street, right in the middle of Kansas City. To say I was amazed would be an understatement. I was accustomed to hearing about certain popular places, such as the Hellfire Club, for example, in New York

City, but New York was far away, so I thought, from Kansas City, Missouri, in attitudes and actions.

I contacted the owner of the Kansas City club and made arrangements to not only interview him, but to spend a couple of days at his place of business, watching, and seeing, what occurred, and what didn't, there. The interviewing process was going to be two parts, before and after I spent time at his business. Part of my agreement was promising to maintain and to guarantee the confidentiality of the clientele.

Although I had seen the world of erotica from almost all angles, this was my first visit to a business or club that was exclusively into B and D, and S and M.

Continued on page 132

Sexy Aunt Mary

I looked forward to my first day doing calls with nervous anticipation. After successfully surviving my first two calls, I figured call number three would be a piece of cake. Little did I realize, yet, how unique everyone's calls were, despite frequently having the same basic desires in the calls. Plus, I had to keep in mind the time element involved with the calls. That was one of the toughest parts of phone sex, working out the time. Since I was an erotic film star, I had a set amount of time for my calls (fifteen minutes). If a person wanted a longer call, it would cost him, but extending the time was not encouraged for the film stars, only for the house girls.

My third call, that first day, was from Ron, in upstate New York. He was in his early forties. His call was based on the younger man-older woman fantasy. He requested that I be his sexy aunt, visiting his family for the summer, and he would be my teenage nephew, about eighteen years old.

Ron had a definite scenario with very specific requests. He had even determined how I should be dressed. Ron said I would be his Aunt Mary.

As his aunt, I have been shopping all day, while he is home all alone. I return about mid-afternoon. Ron doesn't hear my return. I unexpectedly walk into his room with a surprise I had picked up for him. There, I find my own surprise! Ron, my young nephew, is masturbating.

At this point, I seduce him. In the seduction, Ron requests I wear a dressy suit, stockings, hi heels, and very sexy, lacy black underwear; including bra, panties, garter belt, and slip.

When I catch him masturbating, he acts embarrassed. Then, in his scenario, he wants me to respond by being sexually very aggressive.

I come closer to the bed, slowly removing

my clothes, until I get to my underwear. Before I remove my bra and panties, I start sucking him.

Next, he watches me remove my bra and panties, and at that point, he wants his aunt, (me), to insist on fucking him. Finally, to finish off his fantasy, he puts his cock between my breasts, and comes all over them.

It was nice that Ron was quite happy with the call, and said for me to be expecting more calls from him with similar scenarios. However, I found the call an interesting challenge because I had to cover so much ground in a 15-minute time frame. I discovered I was going to have to learn proper pacing with some calls. I figured, rightly, that only experience would resolve that.

* * * *

Smoke Rings

Saul from Fargo, North Dakota, was politically incorrect in his call, but when a person makes these kinds of calls, they are allowed that privilege. Besides, he was a fan of mine, having enjoyed some of my movies.

At the beginning of the call, Saul had lots of questions, but they revolved around one main topic. He wanted to know which porn stars smoked and which did not. Normally, if a person asked this it is because they were not into smoking, and don't want to be around a smoker, intimately. That wasn't the case with Saul. Saul loved to see women smoking, and found it a major turn on. He had one other thing that turned him on, too – oral sex.

After the questions about erotic film stars smoking, Saul is, obviously, very hot. He wants me to talk about performing oral sex on him while I am smoking a cigarette. He even wants me to be holding onto a lit cigarette. Saul asks me to blow smoke rings around his cock. Then, he wants me to continue practicing oral sex on him, while still gripping the cigarette in one hand. Saul has me periodically take drags off it during the performance of the oral sex. It is obvious that this man loves smoking women, literally. Saul is gratified by the very successful call.

I do not smoke in the real world, so I found it a little difficult to do this fantasy, but I did manage to complete it for Saul. In the phone sex world, a person can have their unusual fantasies fulfilled (within a few limitations), in a totally harmless fashion. My lungs did not have to really suffer to make him happy.

* * * *

Bob's Screen Play

I have received lots of unusual calls over the years but this particular one was no doubt one of the most fascinating, as far as being unique. I talked to Bob from Chicago, several times, and he always wanted me to be someone he dreamed about in his fantasies. This time it was somewhat different.

I already knew Bob was bi-sexual and his partner, Paul, was gay, based on what he had told me during previous calls.

On this occasion, Bob called me and wanted me to do a scripted rehearsal with him. The subject of the script was the three of us having dinner, and what occurred after dinner.

I agreed to this extraordinary request, reassuring him that he could certainly enjoy his unusual phone fantasy. He called me twice to go over his script and to discuss changes. I thought, perhaps, he had another fantasy, which he did not mention, of being an x-rated movie director!

Finally, he made arrangements for the officially scripted call.

Bob's special phone fantasy begins with the

three of us meeting at a French restaurant for drinks and dinner. Paul, Bob's lover, leaves the table briefly to go to the men's room. That is the introduction to Bob's following script:

Bob: "Barbara, we've known each other for many years and you know how I feel about you."

Barbara: " Yes, I know, Bob, but I really don't want to get involved with a friend."

Bob: "All I want is to go down on you...that's all I have ever wanted."

Barbara: " Well I'll have to think about it. What will Paul have to say about you doing that?"

Bob: "He won't care. He knows how I feel about you."

Barbara: "Mmmmmmmmmm. Ok I will let you have your way with me, but first you must do me a favor."

Bob: "Anything -- just name it!"

Barbara: "I want to watch you and Paul making love."

Bob: "Is that all? No problem with me on that!"

Paul comes back from the restroom.

Bob: "Paul, guess what? Barbara has agreed to fulfill that special fantasy of mine, with one catch."

Paul: "Oh, yeah, and what might that be?"

Bob: "Well, she wants to watch us make love to each other."

Paul: "Bob, if this is something you really

want, and I know it is, because that's all you have talked about for years, I'll agree to it."

We have another round of drinks and head for my apartment.

Barbara: "Would you guys like another drink? I've got vodka and scotch."

Bob: "Two vodkas, Barbara."

When I return from getting the drinks, both men are on the couch, naked, and Bob is sucking Paul.

Barbara: "Boy you sure don't waste any time."

Paul is laying back enjoying himself while Bob is on his knees going at it. It isn't long before Paul reaches a climax. Then they reverse positions and Paul is returning the favor to Bob.

Bob: "Barbara, why don't you remove your clothes?"

Barbara: "I will in a minute…. I want to enjoy this for a while."

Soon, Bob gets off, and they both just lie there exhausted.

Bob: "Barbara, come on, take your clothes off, already."

Barbara: "Before I do I want you to do one more thing for me."

Bob: "Okay, what is it?"

Barbara: "I want you two to 69 with each other."

Bob: "Okay."

They both become as one. I watch them for a while, and I get really turned on. I slowly undress *while watching them until I can't stand it any longer. I get next to them on the sofa, and as soon as I lie down, Bob has his tongue all over my clit. I have one leg over the top of the sofa and one on the floor. Bob is in heaven! Paul is watching for a long time. Then, I motion him over to my mouth and I start sucking him until he has a quick orgasm. The whole scene is hot, so I get off (as Barbara), too. I love cumming for Bob -- he is fantastic!*

Bob called again the next day, and said everything went perfect. He even told Paul about his fantasy sex phone call, and Paul, too, was excited by the whole scenario. Bob suggested to Paul that he call me and I would fulfill his fantasy, but he never did. I guess I was the wrong sex. I heard from Bob off and on through the years, and he always had me playing a roll with him. However, Paul was never in it again. I figured Paul put a stop to that, or Bob had taken care of that fantasy for life!

* * * *

The Narcissist

Some phone sex callers have phone sex because

they are totally wrapped up in themselves and in their own bodies. By having phone sex they don't have to deal with the feelings or desires of anybody else, and they can set the stage however they please to get the most from their self-love. They are fascinated with their own selves to the degree that they only have a need to satisfy their narcissistic desires. These people love to receive adoration and admiration continuously from any potential lovers, or anyone else, for that matter. True narcissists rarely have long term, fulfilling intimate relationships because they have such an exaggerated love for themselves that there is little room for seriously loving others. However, their phone sex calls were always fascinating and fun.

My first of many calls with Greg, a real estate developer, from New York, is intriguing. When I, initially, ask him to describe himself, and to tell me what he likes, I am given an inkling where we might be going with this call. Greg tells me he has a 43-inch chest, 33-inch waist, is 6 feet 2 inches tall, with blue eyes and blonde hair, and he emphasizes he has a very tight ass. He proceeds to tell me he loves all tight asses.

Then, unexpectedly, he tells me he loves Randy West and Mike Ranger, well-known erotic film actors, because of their great, tight asses. He continues to tell me about having mirrors all over his home and in his bedroom, and even on the ceiling above his bed, so that he can admire his own beautiful ass any time he's home. Next, Greg talks about his underwear. He says he feel his smooth, white balls easily being pulled up. Greg states that as a sideline he loves to pose nude for artists, and he, also, models bikinis, including G-string bikinis.

Greg goes on about how he loves both women and men to admire his oiled-down body, which he thinks is the height of sensuality. He also talks about his bodybuilding.

Finally, he asks me to tell him how much I like his body. He encourages me to say wonderful things about his body, and he asks me to tell him how terrific he looks in his g-string bikini. Greg makes it clear he wants to hear compliments galore and total admiration of his buns and body. While I am doing the complimenting and admiring, I hear him becoming more and more turned on, until he finally gets off.

I found it interesting that there was not any sex in my call with Greg, nor did he expect me to do anything sexual during the call. However, he became fully aroused as the call progressed. Actually, he did more talking than I, by his choice. I was his admiring listener. He enthusiastically described himself to me and basked in my praise in an exaggeratedly, sexual reaction. Calls with Greg were always entertaining and satisfying for him, yet there never was any actual phone sex between us when we talked.

* * * *

The Power of Tits

One afternoon, I received a call from Todd, who worked heavy construction in the Atlantic City area. Todd said he once saw me on stage, and was mesmerized by both my tits and me. He was into big tits, heavy dominance, and pain, he continued.

I wasn't sure where Todd was heading, but since he was doing all the talking, I just went along for the ride.

Todd did not waste a lot of time on pleasantries. Immediately, he was ready for his phone fantasy, during which he called me Mistress Jody. His phone fantasy was the following scenario.

We are in a lesbian bar, called The Redhead, which has a half-circular stage. Todd is sitting on stage, in an armless chair, with his hands tied behind him. I am bare-breasted, standing next to him, while giving instructions to four of my naked, big-breasted girlfriends. He puts up fifty dollars for each girl in this "fantasy boxed-out," as he calls it. Also, he wants it done to loud rock and roll music. With the girls all wearing boxing gloves, Todd wants them to take turns hitting him

they can. If he gives in they win the money. If he doesn't, I, as Mistress Jody, win the money.

How did it end? Well, my character won the money, naturally. Todd also won, from his perspective. He was only lucky that some of my friends, like Annie Sprinkle, weren't involved. With her strength, and her big, bouncing breasts distracting him, she would have cold-cocked him, for sure.

Todd called other times over the years, and his fantasies were virtually always the same, as was his reaction. However, the first time, I was a little startled, to say the least, by this novel call. In fact, how he got off was beyond me, but he did. Obviously, I figured, he enjoyed the test of pain and the nearness of large bouncing boobs!

* * * *

The Cold Architect

The first time Robert called me it was a cold, snowy night, at least in Salt Lake City, where he was! Robert was sitting in front of his fireplace having a

Hot Toddy, when he called. He started out by chatting about himself.

According to his own description, he had brown hair, and dark blue eyes. He said he was an architect, who moved to the mountains and left steamy New Orleans behind, when he and his wife split up. Robert loved the cold, the snow, and the mountains. Plus, he was only an airplane ride away from anywhere he needed to be on business. He talked about his career and the major chains for which he had designed buildings. He had even designed some shopping centers throughout the country, as well.

Although it was apparent that Robert enjoyed visiting with me, he finally began talking about more heated matters. He told me he was fond of big breasts, and he didn't like looking at spread shots of women in magazines. He preferred the softer pinup shots, although he loved to look at big, bare tits. Also, Robert described his penis as "fat."

I could tell Robert was having fun talking about everything with me, but, at last, he was ready for some hot talk.

Robert wants the two of us to be on his bed. He plays with my breasts and, then, I suck him. Following that, he requests that we fuck. He wants me on top, so he can grab my breasts and suck them, at the same time. He, then, turns me over and fucks me briefly with him on top.

Next, he pulls out and strokes his cock over me, while I am lying on my back and he is on his knees. He desires for me to watch him and tell him how to stroke himself, the length of the stroke, the grasp, the speed, everything he does. Mostly, though, he wants me to watch him. He asks me to tell him when to cum as he continues stroking himself. When I sense he is about to explode, I have him cum. He immediately climaxes.

As was typical of many of my callers, Robert liked the woman on top when having intercourse. I had discovered there was a high request for this position. In spite of similarities with others though, I realized Robert's fantasies were uniquely his own. Robert became a regular caller for the next few years, especially during cold winter nights.

Continued from page 119

I met the owner at his establishment, which he called a "club." However, I gathered it was easy to join. He gave me a quick tour, and introduced me to the "mistresses," and, then, we headed to a local coffee shop where we could get a private table, so I could interview him. My interview ended up being lengthy, but my top curiosities were why he had started this business in Kansas City, and how was business.

He told me he had been previously connected to

adult theatres, and also had owned massage parlors. While in those businesses he had met a lot of people who expressed a deep interest in these kinds of sexual happenings. He researched it, visited similar places in other cities, and found out that legally it was actually a lot safer than his massage parlors. Then, he started talking to lots of Kansas Citians, and he discovered what I, too, had found out, since I had gotten in the world of erotica.

People would suddenly tell their most intimate secrets and / or fantasies to me, who would never have dreamed of doing that before I became an erotic film star. Not only strangers, but also people I had known my entire life, would tell me things for which they thought others would criticize them.

Well, because of the nature of his careers, and his easy-going style, people would talk to him, too, giving him the necessary feedback he needed to make his decision to open The Fantasy House.

Regarding business, the response was excellent. He had a very large membership, which was still growing. People were willing to pay the high prices he charged, as well, to enjoy the more exotic forms of certain kinds of sexuality.

His girls loved the business, also, because they had absolutely no sexual contact with any of his club members. Training them was an interesting highlight, he laughingly told me though. Furthermore, he said that not all girls were of the temperament, looks, or personality, to be a dominatrix or mistress. He very carefully chose his personnel, he stated.

When the interview was over for the day, I made

arrangements to come to The Fantasy House the next two days, and watch it in action. I agreed that if a member did not want me present, I would go to another room during whatever occurred with that member. Any clientele, who was there, when I was present, would be told the truth that I was writing a story about the business for a magazine.

The follow day, I arrived as the place was opening in the morning. There were several female staff already present, who greeted me warmly. They were all good looking and personable. Of course, the ladies were dressed in typical dominatrix outfits, lots of black leather and studs, black stockings and high heels or boots.

As I knew the owner was not going to be present, I freely chatted with the girls. Unanimously, they told me how much they liked working there. They also said they got really nice tips too, in addition to great pay. The girls said the police came in sometimes, undercover, and had a session, but it didn't matter because they were not breaking any laws.

One girl, a stunning blonde, told me one day an undercover officer came in that she recognized from her previous job, but he didn't seem to recognize her. She didn't care for him, she said, so she was really happy when he asked for a spanking. She bound his ankles and wrists to a table, after he undressed, except for his boxer shorts. The police officers never removed their underwear, according to her. She then proceeded to give him the spanking of his life, she laughingly told me. He finally begged for mercy, but she pretended she thought it was part of his fantasy, so she initially ignored him.

I have to admit I felt sorry for the officer, because I didn't think that was something he would have picked to do by choice. She said he seemed mad when he left, and he didn't tip her. I didn't wonder why!

Every once in a while officers would come in, in uniform, for about a minute, take a quick look and leave quickly, too. The girls said the uniformed ones were always nice and polite to them.

Some of the girls had previously worked for the owner in his other establishments, but they thought this was so much better. The girls told me they never touched a man's genitals. If they did they would get fired. Plus, overall, the clientele was very nice, they claimed.

The female manager, (no males worked there), took me on a tour of their establishment, which looked like a house between two office buildings, in midtown. There were strange tables with holes in them, racks, harnesses, clips, various whips, leather straps, all kinds of fun things. I did not really know what some of the things were, actually.

Then, there was a little room done in all pink, which had a dressing table, cosmetics, a freestanding, full-length mirror, and a closet. This room, which I thought of as the pink room, was where men who wanted to cross-dress for an hour or so could have fun. The closet was filled with all sorts of sexy, very feminine clothing in sizes that would normally fit men. There were hi heels, stockings, and bras and panties, as well. The girls would put make up on the men and fuss with them, like they were their girlfriends. They would help the guys dress, and carry on, as if they were just a bunch of the girls. They even had wigs for the men who wanted them. There was a table set up in the pink room, with tea cups and all, for the men who wanted to go that route, too, while dressed as females.

The girls discussed their clientele with me in general terms. Confidentiality was the top rule with them, I was informed. They claime
their club members were prominent citizens, and told me to not be shocked if I recognized anyone.

Of course, they didn't know what everyone did who came there, but they knew about plenty of them. There were a couple of bank presidents, they said, and one was expected while I was going to be present. They had heads of businesses and other kinds of executives, who came to the club. Some military people, who were in positions of power, were on their membership list. They had at least one professional athlete, who was a member, as well. Naturally, there were regular working guys, too, but it seemed by what they said that the bosses were the primary clientele.

I asked them if they had any idea why. The manager told me that many had given them reasons, and they were always essentially the same. The pressures of calling the shots, making the decisions, always ordering others around, took its toll. For a brief period, they would come here, be called names and told what to do, be punished, or humiliated. The men found mental and sexual release through the experiences.

Continued

Crotchless Panties

Frequently, there were calls from men who liked talking with erotic film stars because they felt comfortable enough to share their most secret fantasies, actions, desires, with the stars, and not worry about being judged by them. I received such a call, one evening, from Craig, who lived in Phoenix. Craig had previously talked to some other stars before I had come on board, but I was clueless to their past conversations.

At first, Craig simply chatted with me, as a prelude to getting into his desires. He told me he was an executive in a large company, which didn't surprise me, because he sounded pleasant and intelligent. Craig talked about the high stress level in his job and how our kind of conversation relaxed him. Finally, he got to the purpose of his call.

Craig tells me he loves to be sucked and he loves to fuck, but most of all he loves anal sex. He continues, saying that he, also, loves to watch

a woman use dildos on herself. He likes to see her use them anally as well as in her pussy. Then, Craig reveals what he feels is his most intimate secret. He loves to wear silky red crotchless panties, especially when he's having erotic thoughts, and always when he has a fantasy phone call!

Craig informs me that he always leaves them on for the sex part of the call. He wishes he could do that in his real life because he feels more sexually satisfied when he orgasms while wearing his crotchless panties. He makes comments to me, which I perceive as indicating that he wishes me to admire him in them. Of course, I do, and his reaction is immediate. He becomes very hot!

Now, Craig asks me to suck him, (his panties on for the entire fantasy, naturally). After sucking him, he requests that I sit on his cock. Then, he requests that I suck him again. While doing that, I squeeze his buttocks with my hands, and that causes him to suddenly explode in orgasm.

I knew Craig was not alone in having a somewhat unusual desire in his sexual fantasies. I had already discovered that, frequently, men with high-level, stressful jobs had desires that were not always what one would expect. I was growing accustomed to expecting the unexpected from my callers.

Craig told me how much he enjoyed the call, and would definitely call again in two to three weeks. He, also, said he hoped he could hold out until we had anal sex, in his fantasy, the next time. Approximately two weeks later, he called as promised.

* * * *

The Round Bed Hang-Up

Late one evening, I received a call from Herb, who was a police officer at a juvenile detention center in Pittsburgh, Pennsylvania. Herb told me that his job was full of headaches and he liked to kick back in the evenings. Tonight he wanted to kick back with me.

Herb told me he wasn't much of a drinker, but occasionally liked a cocktail. He, also said he was a tit man. Herb especially loved nice, big, natural breasts. He enjoyed playing with them, sucking them, and fucking them.

Referring to himself as a "shy exhibitionist," Herb said that he desired to get naked with a lady in an oversized, round bed. At the same time, he was always nervous being naked around a woman. As a result, he felt extremely vulnerable.

Then, Herb told me he wanted to have sex with me on a giant, round bed.

In the phone fantasy, Herb fixes cocktails for us, Tom Collins for him and Lancers for me. We go into his bedroom, which has his favorite play area in it -- a king-sized round bed. We briefly make out, necking and kissing. Suddenly, I rip off his clothes, and remove mine, too. Then, I lick his nipples. I sit on his cock. After that, I suck him, and he follows the sucking by fucking my breasts. Finally, he has me go down on him again, and that sets him off.

Even before Herb climaxed, he kept telling me he was cumming, over and over. When he actually did orgasm, he let out one final yell that he was cumming. Then, abruptly, he hung up.

From the beginning of the call, Herb had been pleasant and courteous, although not particularly talkative. However, after he completed the purpose of his call, he did what a small percentage of callers would do. He hung up on me. When I checked around, I discovered that this happened even more frequently to the regular girls who did fantasy phone sex calls. While I found it disconcerting, I learned to accept the fact that some callers just couldn't say good-bye after that high level of arousal. At least, I was prepared if Herb called again.

* * * *

The Milk Man

New callers to phone sex were always exciting, because I never knew what to expect, and they generally didn't have a clue either. Late one night, I received a call from a brand new member, who was a total virgin to fantasy phone sex. Charles, from Cincinnati, was a company supervisor, who had been partying earlier that night, with co-workers. He came home and found himself feeling sexy. He decided this was the night to go for it, to call Personal Services and to talk to me!

Charles told me he had seen me in magazines and he had read my columns. He was intrigued by me, although he had never seen any of my movies. At this point, he was ready to share his turn ons or fantasies with me.

Eating pussy and practicing oral-anal sex on a woman were the first two things Charles mentioned that he loved to do to a woman. He continued on, telling me he was crazy about being sucked, and he loved to suck large breasts. Then, he said his number one, all-time turn on was something he had experienced only once. He loved to suck big breasts full of milk, and loved to taste the milk, and have them squirt all over his face. He said nothing in the world excited him more than that.

By this time, Charles was definitely ready for fantasy phone sex. He wanted some of these turn ons included, but warned me he was so hot already that he didn't think he could get too many in on this call.

Charles' fantasy begins with him licking my pussy and tonguing me. He sucks my breasts and he loves it. He wishes to fantasize he is milking my breasts (although I didn't really have milking breasts). In his fantasy, I squirt milk on his face and he licks it up. Then, I begin sucking him. He is so turned on, that I barely mention it and he cums!

Although Charles was new to phone sex, and called at a very late hour, he adjusted quickly to it. He chatted briefly after his orgasm, telling me how great it was, and how much he looked forward to more calls.

* * * *

Soldier Boy

Daryl, from Chicago, called late one February

night, with a desire to get as far away as possible from his stressful career and all its responsibilities. He was the President of a large financial institution, and he wanted to escape from his ever-constant, decision-making world, for a little while. Daryl felt his fantasies were somewhat different and could endanger his career if he ever treated them other than as fantasies. Since he was familiar with me, he decided to give me a call and fulfill one of his fantasies, on the phone, in a safe fashion.

The kinds of fantasies that turned Daryl on, were more common, in various forms, than he realized. Frequently, men in power, I had discovered, had fantasies that put them in totally, non-decision making positions, regardless of the variables.

On this night, Daryl wanted to be a teenage boy attending a military school. He had distinct ideas what he wanted to occur, and went through the details with me before we began. Also, Daryl wanted me to play myself in his fantasy.

Daryl is a senior high school student at a military academy in the south. He is off school grounds, with his friends, but is in his uniform.

I am starring in a funny, yet, sexy stage show, in town.

He and his friends walk by the theatre as I am coming out, so, they stop to talk to me. The friends finally walk on, but Daryl lingers. I think he is cute and invite him over to my suite.

When we get to my suite, it's obvious that he is very nervous and somewhat in awe. I order us some lemonade from room service to help him relax. While we are waiting for the lemonade, I have him sit on a large, red, plush couch. After it arrives, I come sit next to him. I take his hand and put it on my breasts. Then, I take off my black silk blouse and black lacy bra and push his head down on my breasts and I tell him to suck them. He nervously does this, as I give him instructions on how to do it. He figures it out pretty quickly.

After he masters the breast sucking, I make him lay back on the couch. Now, I get up and slowly pull off my skirt. I order him to pull my panties down, which he quickly does. Then, I straddle his face and give him lessons on cunnilingus. While he is eating me, I reach behind a couch cushion and pull out a dildo, which I hand him. I tell Daryl to insert it in me and to use it on me. Daryl is more than happy to obey. As he does this, I reach down and grab his very hard cock through his uniform pants, but I don't do anything to him. He is my pleasure slave, at this point.

When I am satiated, I have him remove the dildo and I get dressed. I tell him to stay on the couch until I return shortly.

I come back in a few minutes with a bunch of his friends, and other fellow students. At this time, I command Daryl to unzip his pants, pull out his cock, and masturbate in front of this group of boys and me.

As he is jerking off, the other boys laugh and ridicule him. He finally cums while he's kneeling at my feet. I order Daryl to scream when he cums, which he enthusiastically does.

This was a convoluted fantasy, but it was exactly what Daryl wanted. As was frequently the case, Daryl was typical of many of the callers, in the sense, that he had his own ideas, his own scenario, he wanted played out. I fulfilled his wishes and he was relaxed and totally mellow when we finally said good-bye.

* * * *

The Spandex Man

A Scottsdale, Arizona, man, named Frank, called me, on an early April evening, desiring to share his fantasy with me. First, though, Frank wanted to talk briefly about himself. He told me he was involved with architecture. He also was single and traveled a great deal. Frank said he was 6 feet 1 inch tall, had baby blue eyes, and a great body. He even described his penis, as being about eight inches long, thick, and having a "big, purple head," as he put it.

Before we began Frank's phone fantasy, he told me he was into spandex. It thrilled him to look at women dressed in spandex, and to touch women covered well, because he found that a real turn on.

At the start of Frank's phone sex fantasy, he requested I wear tight purple spandex slacks, a sheer see through blouse, and a black bra and panties. He told me he had on spandex bikini underwear.

In the fantasy, Frank meets me for a drink at a cocktail lounge. I'm sitting on a stool at the bar. He's standing right next to me. While we are having our drinks, he rubs my ass with his hands, feeling the spandex pants on me. He runs a hand across my thigh. He brushes an arm against my breasts. He admires my bra, which he can see quite well, through my very sheer blouse. I can feel the nudge of his hard cock through his pants as he pushes it against my ass.

Finally, we leave the bar, and go to his condo. He is touching me through my clothing the whole way there.

When we arrive at the condo, we immediately go to the bedroom, where he has a king size waterbed, covered with black satin sheets. He desires I leave on my clothes, but he does ask me to lie back on the bed. He kisses me tenderly, while, at the same time, he is running his hands all over me feeling me through the spandex. Frank spreads my legs and rubs my crotch through the tight, sexy slacks. He plays with my breasts through my blouse and bra. Then, he slowly unbuttons my blouse, and unfastens my bra. Initially, Frank kisses my "pretty tits," and after that, gently tongues my pussy.

Next, Frank lies back on the bed, and I feel his cock and testicles through his spandex bikini underwear. I pull his undies off slowly, licking as I do, until I, finally, suck his cock. Before long, we fuck with me on top, so he can lightly nibble on my breasts, at the same time. Then, we fuck sideways, until suddenly Frank has a bursting orgasm.

Frank wasn't the only man, with whom I talked, who was into spandex. There were others who also found some kind of sexual, pleasurable enhancement from spandex playing a part in their fantasies.

The phone sex fantasy was an obvious success, and Frank was extremely pleased. I talked with him many times over the next few years.

* * * *

Peeping-Tom Fantasy

A slightly different call came from Marty, a businessman from Albany, New York. Marty described himself as being an average looking guy, five feet seven inches, with brown hair and brown eyes. Initially, he tells me he loves big breasts. However, the more we chatted, I discovered he was into several other things, including dominance. He made it clear though, he did not care for pain. Marty also said that he was turned on by seeing a woman in stockings. Then, he added that he had a Peeping-Tom fantasy that he would like to fulfill. He already had ideas about what he wanted in his phone sex fantasy.

I am on the phone with my girlfriend Betsy. We are comparing notes on lovers. I get turned on and start playing with my breasts and my pussy. I have on stockings, hi heels, and a garter belt, having removed rest of my clothing while talking to Betsy. As I continue playing with myself, I become aware that a man is watching me through a window. I get more turned on and continue intimately handling myself.

Finally, I decide to invite my Peeping Tom inside. It's apparent he's very hot and horny. I order him to kiss my shoes. He immediately does. Then, I tell him to kiss and lick my stockinged legs up to my knees. After that, I instruct him to suck my tits. Then, I demand he eat my pussy and use a vibrator on me, at the same time.

I know there is a young man, about eighteen, and very pretty, doing yard work next door. I get up and call to him from the window, and invite him inside, as well. While I do not permit Marty to fuck me, I do suggest to the yardman that he fuck me instead. I tell Marty to watch.

After the yardman is finished, I order Marty to jerk off on my breasts. He happily fulfills my demand.

Marty was quick to give a positive response to all my requests throughout his fantasy. It was obvious he loved it. We had done the various things he had requested. Although Marty implied the Peeping Tom fantasy was only a fantasy, I wondered if he had ever been a Peeping Tom, in reality. However, I never did ask him.

Marty did make one other request from me before we hung up. He asked me if I could have a male slave present while we were having a phone session, sometime. Of course, I gave the appropriate answer, for him. I told him I would think about it. I did hear from Marty again.

Continued from page 136

I asked about the sexual part since the girls didn't have contact with any penises. The guys would either jerk off or just orgasm without anyone touching them, including themselves. Sometimes, guys wouldn't get off, nor wanted to get off, but they were happy because of the mental release.

The prices were not cheap either. For the simplest, quickest happening, the cost started at three figures and climbed. I realized this definitely was not a poor guy's hobby. Some men came in almost daily, too, I was informed.

Finally, a client walked in and I watched the manager take care of the business part. This man wanted his usual, he said. Then, he immediately headed for the pink room. I followed at a distance, knowing that I was dressed like an outsider, and not wishing to freak the man out.

The girls decided not to introduce me by name, at my suggestion, and just stated the purpose of my visit. He readily agreed to my presence as long as I didn't mention his real name.

That was easy, as I didn't know his real name because the girls were already calling him a female name, Amanda.

He slipped behind a screen and took off his suit and underwear. One of the girls, the one he requested, knew his tastes and sizes already. They had coded cards for different members with that kind of information on them.

She handed him a black garter belt and silk panties and bra, which he put on behind the screen. Then he came out and sat at the dressing table. The girl, Julie, helped him put on stockings. Then, she complimented him on how sexy he looked. He got up and admired himself in the full-length mirror.

Next, came the makeup. It was the full works. She

him.

He wanted to wear a slip, so she found him a black, nylon, full-length one. After that, the two picked out a dress for him. It was a nice looking black number. All the client needed were the hi heels. Amazingly, Julie had a pair that fit him.

After they were finished, he stood in front of the mirror and preened for a while. He visited with Julie and with me; and he walked around as if he were a model, arching his back and swaying his hips. Clearly, Amanda was having a good time. Finally, though, it was time for his fantasy to end.

Julie cleaned his face of makeup and he went behind the screen and changed his clothes. When he came back out he was all man again. He was very happy, giving Julie a hefty tip, and shaking hands with me. Then, he was gone.

When he was shaking hands with me, I noticed he had on a wedding ring. After he left, I was informed most of the men who came in for the cross-dressing were married. His use of the pink room was pretty typical as well, according to Julie.

Members continued coming throughout the day, and surprisingly, no one complained about my presence. In some cases I think the men enjoyed the audience. The majority of them wanted to be called insulting, put-down names and either to be spanked or whipped. Generally, they were bound spread eagle on the table face down or spread eagle on the rack. Whatever they chose they were at the mercy of the dominatrix. Most of the men were naked. A few left on their underwear during their sessions. I also found out the purpose of the hole in the table.

When the men laid on their stomachs they were supposed to put their penises in the hole. That way, if they got an erection it didn't have to be adjusted, and if they got off, while in that situation, they ended up shooting their sperm on the floor below the table. Some men really did cum like that. Other men who left on their underwear came in their shorts.

One man, who came in, was a Master Sergeant, in the military. He was a big guy, tough-looking, with a military haircut. He had a standing appointment every week. His desires were similar to the others but he had one little oddity, it seemed to me. Initially, he liked to be hooked up to the table, naked, and called names, teased, provoked, and he loved to be spanked until his butt was red. So far, he had been more or less like the others.

Then, something a little different occurred. His dominatrix called in another girl, and the two of them sat down on each side of him and proceeded to play tit tat toe on his back with their fingernails, deliberately cutting him with each line, circle, and x, so each mark bled. They continued playing games all over his back until his entire back was bleeding. The Master Sergeant was immensely enjoying it. I took a peak under the table, and saw their bloodletting game had really turned him on. Finally, he yelled out and orgasmed as they were finishing their last game.

His back was completely bloody, but he was thrilled. The girls explained to me after he left that it was important to him that he be made to bleed; that was his special request. His dominatrix had done various things to make him bleed, but playing games on him had become her favorite way. Besides, he loved it, she said. I saw she was right.

The next day was essentially the same; men would come in and happily suffer, get off, and leave. I did some mental math calculations, too. They had taken in a lot of money in those two days!

Following my two days, I met with the owner again, and he suggested that due to its success he might open many Fantasy House establishments.

Continued on page 169

Water Sports

Occasionally, I would hear from callers with highly unusual interests, untypical of the large variety of desires that pleased most my callers. Some house girls had "specialties," for which they would receive most their calls. An example would be Heather, a medical student at U.C.L.A., who did calls as a dominatrix. Her calls were almost entirely composed of submissives. The specialties were generally not the case with the erotic film stars, who did calls, however. We talked to a mixed bag of fans, ardent admirers, people who were interested in our looks, or some area of our expertise, or anyone else who desired to talk to us because they knew we were for real. As a result, we had to be careful not to get complacent thinking we had heard everything. Speaking for myself, I constantly thought about being prepared for most kinds of calls.

Still, no matter how prepared I was, I would sometimes be surprised by the nature of a call. Regardless of my career in eroticism, there were areas that personally were not of interest to me. When I received such a call devoted to a non-appealing subject, I would summon my acting skills to assist me. I did not, nor would not, judge a call, or caller, for his eccentric desires, as long as no one was hurt by those desires. Nonetheless, there definitely were calls that did not entice or attract me.

I received such a call, late one night, from Norman. Immediately, Norman told me he loved big tits, and sexy lingerie, which was not unusual to me. I received lots of calls from "breast men," and most men liked sexy lingerie.

Norman continued, telling me he also loved to wear women's lingerie and that he was a closet cross-dresser. He said it turned him on feeling soft, silky fabric against his skin. In fact, Norman told me he was wearing blue silk women's panties, while we were talking.

Then, Norman got to the crux of his fantasy call. Norman told me he was into "golden showers." He went on to say that he loved to pee in his panties, and that he loved to pee on his girlfriend and she peed back on him. He added he loved to piss in his bed.

Now, that Norman had worked himself up, he said he wanted to tell me a tale about him and his girlfriend, Jan. That would be his phone sex fantasy, sharing his story with me.

Norman told me, one evening, he and Jan are wearing matching silk blue panties. They are in bed, feeling each other up. He briefly plays with her breasts, and sucks them, while she strokes his cock through his sexy silk undies. At the same time, Norman fingers Jan's pussy through her panties. Eventually, they remove each other's panties. At this point, they fuck, but with Jan sitting on his cock, in a squatting position. They fuck in that position until Jan cums. When she finishes cumming, she lifts up but is still in a squatting position, and she pisses all over Norman's cock and balls.

Norman said that Jan, then, takes his hand and puts it on his wet-from-piss cock. She requests he jerks himself off that way. She watches him, stroking his very wet cock, until he cums. When Norman tells me about cumming, it instantly sets him off. Immediately, he cums over the phone!

I could tell Norman felt really great after his orgasm. His enjoyment for "golden showers" was obvious, and was something in which he took maximum pleasure. Based on what he told me about his girlfriend, this kind of sex was lots of fun for her, too. I wished the two of them lots of future pleasure, together, as we said our good byes.

* * * *

Cross-Dresser

I was relaxing at home one evening when Laci, a screener, called to tell me she had something of an unusual call for me. She said the caller was one of the oldest members of Personal Services Club.

I asked in what way was he one of the oldest?

Laci told me she meant both in age and as one of the original callers from Personal Services Club's inception.

I did not see anything different about any of that. If anything, I thought it was nice to be able to talk to an older, long-time member, I commented.

Laci agreed with me, but added that wasn't to what she was referring. Then, she explained.

My caller, Harold, from Joliet, Illinois, was sometimes Harold when he called and other times he was Wilma. She said the screeners were supposed to ask him how he was feeling, and who he was, each time he called. She added he was a cross-dresser, and a very sweet man. Laci also warned me that several years previous, he had had an epileptic seizure while on the phone with one of the girls. She managed to get the attention of the manager who called 911, in Illinois, and an ambulance got there in time. Laci said he had been very careful with his medications ever since, but she wanted me to have a heads-up since I was going to be having the call from home.

My immediate question was who was Harold that night?

Laci informed me he was Wilma, and I was to be sure and address him as Wilma from the beginning of the call.

Following my chat with the screener, I immediately called Wilma. She answered on the first ring. After introducing myself, and exchanging pleasantries, Wilma told me she had read about me and admired my erotic abilities, and she wished she could learn to do my oral techniques.

Then, Wilma abruptly changed the subject, and asked me if she looked pretty in her pink silk panties and camisole, and her nice make up, including pink lipstick that matched her outfit. Of course, I told her she looked divine.

She continued, telling me about a book she had been reading that evening, and how it made her cock really hard. She said she would like to tell me about the book, which she then did. She also made it clear it was her fantasy.

The general idea of the book was a man owned a manufacturing company in some small town. His beautiful blond son goes off to college and becomes a member of the track team. He misses his son, so he goes to a track meet as a surprise. His son doesn't know he is there. When the meet finishes, his son immediately takes off. Dad follows him and sees him go into a black man's cottage, which happens to be the college's head gardener's home. Dad is curious, so he peeks in the window and sees his fair-haired son on his knees being fucked in the ass by the gardener.

As Wilma is going into the details of this book, her breathing becomes faster and more audible. When she reaches the point about what dad sees in the window, Wilma lets out a yelp and a moan. I immediately knew Wilma had orgasmed.

Following Wilma's orgasm, she wanted to converse for a little while. She told me when she was in high school she met a college boy, Sonny, who seduced her. She instantly fell in love with Sonny. Sonny made Wilma into his "little woman." Of course, Wilma was strictly Harold in those days, but he didn't care what he was called as long as he was Sonny's little woman.

The "love affair" continued for a few years. Sonny taught Harold/Wilma to be a submissive. Wilma said she always obeyed Sonny, and he taught her everything about sex and pleasing the partner. She would do anything for Sonny. When Sonny finally ended it with her, it broke her heart. It was sometime after that, when Wilma first appeared. Wilma said she had had many lovers over the years, but none ever compared to Sonny, either physically or in her heart.

As Wilma was now ready to go to bed for the night, she ended the call telling me how much she enjoyed talking with me, and she would love to tell me about more of her books. She said she would be calling me again.

After we hung up, I thought about Wilma and her fantasies, and I wondered what would happen on the nights that Harold showed up. I knew Wilma, or Harold, or both, would be calling me again. I figured I would be in for some more surprises. Wilma was very nice, so I could not help wonder what Harold would be like. It was a unique call, but it was only the first of many calls I received from Harold/Wilma.

* * * *

Shoelace Fetish

Occasionally a call would come from someone who could probably be thought of as a fetishist, because he was into a particular body part to the extreme, and wanted that part in an unusual way. Sometimes, that caller would slightly cross over into other areas, like domination or / and bondage, at the same time, to fulfill his fantasy involving that particular body part. If a screener knew the caller was generally into this kind of fantasy, she was very good about letting me know.

One night, I received a call of this nature from Evan, of Richmond, Virginia. Evan said he was a reasonably good-looking six-footer, with thick, wavy, dark brown hair, and green eyes. He was in his mid-thirties.

When I got Evan on the phone, he told me he had been admiring my picture in a magazine, just before the call. He added he was crazy about my "pretty" nipples, and that he was hoping I was in an outrageous mood.

Evan begins his phone sex fantasy by telling me he wishes to suck on my nipples, and to get them really hard. Then, he takes a pair of thin black shoelaces and ties them tight around my hard nipples.

Next, Evan takes more shoelaces and ties my wrists behind my back. He continues by tying my legs to my waist, to not only spread my legs wide, but also to pull them up, which exposes my "cunt" more than simply being tied spread eagle, he said.

After he gets me tied up to his pleasing, he sucks my nipples, again, and he eats my cunt.

Now, Evan sticks his cock in my mouth and has me suck him. He does all the guiding and holding of his cock, since I'm still tied up.

Evan is very worked up and breathing hard. So, he takes the two shoelaces on the nipples and ties them together, bringing my breasts closer to each other. Next, Evan takes the other ends of those same two shoelaces and puts them behind my neck, halter style, and ties them tight, pulling my breasts up toward my face. He does this, he says, to make it easier to suck them, while he fucks me. At this point, Evan does fuck me in this position, successfully sucking my breasts at the same time, according to him. He describes all his tying up actions, repeatedly, as he gets even hotter. Finally, Evan has a strong orgasm while we are fucking.

Following his orgasm, Evan was very polite and courteous. He talked about untying me as soon as the sex was over, and how much he appreciated me doing this phone sex fantasy with him.

Actually, Evan was very nice, especially considering the nature of his unusual fantasy. The tied-up nipples were the most important part to him. He was a nipple lover above all other parts of a woman, but he always wanted them to be tied nipples. There was never any variation on that part of his fantasy. That was what the screener had told me, when she called previous to his and my conversation. This particular part of Evan's fantasy did not differ in his call that night, nor in later calls, with me, either.

Evan was at least a partial fetishist, but was it of nipples, shoelaces, or a combination? I was never really sure, but I knew that he always had the two together, whenever I spoke with him during the next few years.

* * * *

Surgery Dilemma

In the very early hours, one January morning, I received a call from Wes, a talker from Tampa, Florida. Wes told me he was with a large radio station, in Tampa, and that he really liked his career. He said, however, he had a tremendous desire to get into a different medium. He wished to be in front of the camera, making movies and videos. Wes felt he had the "right look" that was perfect for the camera.

My curiosity about the looks of this made-for-the-camera man were somewhat satisfied when he described himself as 39 years old, very good looking (according to the ladies, he added), 6 feet tall, 205 pounds, with bright blue eyes and dark brown, wavy hair. Wes also said he was well built.

I asked Wes what kind of movies and videos

he had in mind, assuming he would say comedies, adventures, or something similar. I guessed wrong.

Wes wanted to make a porn movie. He said that was the ultimate fantasy with him, something he badly wanted to do. Then, he continued describing himself to me.

Wes claimed he was extremely well-endowed, with a penis that was not only longer than most, but also was very wide. He did not come across as bragging, but was totally matter of fact about it. Wes had one major concern about his penis though, which he seemed to feel the need to discuss with me.

He told me he was compulsive and obsessive about being clean. This was why he was concerned about his penis. Wes said he was uncircumcised, and it bothered him immensely. He said that he took great care of his penis and kept it very clean, washing it multiple times daily, but it wasn't enough for him. He had gone to the doctor recently to see about getting circumcised at his age. The doctor told him the pros and cons of such surgery, especially at 39. Wes was still trying to make up his mind when he called me.

He asked my opinion.

I wasn't about to express a preference or an opinion and possibly influence this man I had never met, on such an important matter. I suggested he see if he could find others who had had the surgery as an adult, and get their reactions.

Wes continued talking about the world of radio and the world of porn. I mostly listened to Wes, which was actually rather nice at that bewitching hour.

At last, Wes mentioned he loved clean women with

big breasts. He also appreciated full, curvy asses. Mostly, though, he was into tits.

He begins fantasizing that he is with me after a night on the town, in New York City. We are in a suite at the Plaza.

I remove my purple dress and lavender bra. He wants me to move around so he can watch my free breasts moving. Wes requests I even do a little dance so my breasts bounce. Next, I swing them in his face. He catches them and just holds them for a minute. Then, he licks them and sucks them. Ultimately, Wes bites my nipples, fairly gently, but enough for me to notice, he tells me. Biting my nipples brings him to an orgasm.

The phone sex with Wes was brief. He seemed more interested in talking, which was okay because I enjoyed listening to him. However, I did speak long enough to give him some suggestions if he was truly serious about entering into the world of erotic films. After my suggestions, we said our good byes.

* * * *

Milwaukee Brewmaster

Frequently callers wanted to hear stories, or fantasy tales, about sexual experiences between other people and me, as a prelude to their fantasy sex. Sometimes, they were true stories; other times, fiction worked quite well. The callers did not care, as long as it fulfilled their desires.

Dennis, a brewery worker, from a Milwaukee, Wisconsin, suburb, was such a caller, who wished to hear a couple of specific tales preceding his fantasy sex. He had seen both Juliet Anderson and me in **Outlaw Ladies**, and had dreamed of watching us having sex with each other. This called for my creative juices to flow as I fashioned a fictional sexual story about sex between Juliet and me that covered the areas he desired. He wanted to see Juliet and me having oral sex with each other and using dildos, as well. Dennis also asked to see us French kissing.

After that tale, Dennis wished for another similar style story between another girl and me. I made up a second erotic tale for him that had the desired effect. His own juices were building up and getting him primed for his phone sex fantasy by the end of that hot story.

Dennis completely changes scenarios as we begin his fantasy. He requests I tie him up and dominate him with sexual pleasure only. I use my stage stockings to tie him, spread eagle, and

I immediately sit on his face and have him lick my pussy. Then, I move off his face and stick my breasts in his mouth for him to suck. Now, I sit back on his face, and I lean forward and suck his cock while he is eating my pussy. I have another stocking available in which I have tied eleven knots. I rub it all over his balls, and on and off his cock, while I continue sucking him, and he is still eating my pussy. As Dennis is obviously closing in on cumming, I stick the knotted stocking up his ass. I turn around and sit on his cock and fuck him hard, with my right hand holding the end of the stocking. When Dennis starts cumming, I pull the knotted stocking out of his butt hole, simultaneously. He loves it and yells out as he orgasms!

Instantly, after cumming, Dennis hung up on me. The screener had already warned that Dennis always hung up on the person with whom he was talking, so it was not a surprise. He had been polite and reasonably verbal throughout the call, until he came.

Dennis asked for a lot in his call, two stories and a fantasy, yet, he managed to enjoy it all and "get off," all in less time than he was actually allowed. Of course, hanging up abruptly no doubt made a time difference, too.

Dennis did call again, and his desires remained the same. His hanging up record stayed at one hundred percent, as well, throughout the times he talked with me or with anybody else.

* * * *

Nuclear Fantasy

Sometimes I would get calls that took unusual turns during the phone sex fantasy. It might be something the caller didn't want to initially mention, but would suddenly throw in during his heated moments. I would always try to be mentally prepared for these changes, so I could quickly and verbally go the new direction. Nonetheless, it was occasionally a surprise, which was the case with this call.

Harry, a resident of a Providence, Rhode Island, suburb, told me he was a big guy, standing 6 feet 6 inches and weighing 250 pounds, with cobalt blue eyes and dark blond hair. He said he was a supervisor at a nuclear power plant. Harry added that he was a tit and leg man. He loved to caress and lick long, beautiful legs, but nothing was more enjoyable than sucking "big, hard, juicy nipples."

At the beginning of Harry's fantasy phone sex, he has us on his king-sized waterbed. He immediately goes for my legs, stroking and licking them. Harry follows that by avidly going down on me. Next, he moves to his number one pleasure, my nipples, which he squeezes and sucks. I hear

him panting while he is concentrating on my nipples, in his fantasy.

Then, comes the first of Harry's surprises.

He requests I invite Annie Sprinkle, a former erotic film star and a long-time friend of mine, (who was noted for an unusual "talent" in the world of erotica, but her specialty was not in my area of expertise), into his fantasy for a cameo appearance. Harry has specific instructions for Annie's role. He wants Annie to walk in on us, while he continues sucking my nipples. She tells him to stop, which he does. Next, she goes over to him and pees on his body. When she finishes, Harry wants Annie to leave us. So, we tell her goodbye as she disappears from his fantasy.

Now, Harry surprises me with his second unforeseen desire.

Harry requests to fuck me, (no surprise there), and asks that we invite Big Monty in to join us so that he could suck Big Monty while he is fucking me.

Monty quickly joins us, as I do not wish to lose Harry's momentum.

While I am sitting on Harry's cock, Monty is straddling Harry's chest and fucking Harry in the mouth with his swollen, hard cock. At this point, Harry is panting loudly and fast, and seems close to his explosive finale. Big Monty cums while Harry is sucking him, which causes Harry to go off in my pussy, simultaneously.

As Harry slowly got his breath back, he nicely

thanked me for a marvelous time. He told me he had enjoyed me in magazines, but now he was going to buy some of my movies, too.

Harry was an interesting guy, whose fantasy twisted and turned all directions without a single, early clue. In fact, if anything, his lead off comments indicated he had fairly standard or common desires. So, in a sense, Harry got the best of me, because I wasn't expecting either of his surprise wishes during his fantasy. As I was always expecting the unexpected, it was remarkable to me that he unknowingly pulled a "gotcha" on me. Since he was a very nice guy, I laughed to myself after we hung up, thinking, "Point one to you, Harry!" However, I knew if I had any more calls with him that would be his only score. After all, it was my home court.

Continued from page 153

At a later date, I was asked by a different magazine to do a story on a B and D place of business located in California. This one was named The Chateau after Le Chateau from the ***Story of O,*** the famous French erotic novel, written by Pauline Réage.

Actually, The first Chateau was located in the Los Angeles area, and had been so successful the owner opened a second one in San Francisco. That was the place I was asked to visit.

When I arrived at The Chateau, I discovered it was a large, roomy place in a middle class area of San Francisco. Upon ringing the bell, I was greeted by a stud, who happened to also be the manager. He went by the name Sir James, like the lead male character in the ***Story of O.***

Sir James introduced me to the leather-dressed, good looking dominatrixes and the fluffy-dressed, cute submissives. There were both at this place, although most clients were interested in being submissive themselves. However, because they allowed the girls to play the role of submissives, there was always a male on the premises, who always remained quietly present in the room for those particular appointments.

Again, like The Fantasy House, the ladies did not touch the men's genitals. They supplied prophylactics to the men if they wanted them. Otherwise, the men would have to fend for themselves if they orgasmed.

The Chateau had a lot of equipment, in addition to the prerequisite tables with the holes in them. They had the racks, of course, and a circular upside down item, which could also be raised up in the air. There were objects that looked like they could have been centuries old, and were pretty painful and weird looking to my inexpert eyes.

Sir James showed me their supply room, and it was a most amazing site. The locked, storage room was huge, and completely filled with all kinds of devises, including an incredible number of every possible kind of whip. It had chains, ropes, nipple clips, leather, latex, bands, underwear, handcuffs, cock rings, ball pullers, dildos, dog collars, etc. There were strap-on dildos, of which I wondered about the use in this environment. However, I was informed they were not to be used on the clientele, but for effect only, or for little "skits" two girls might do on rare occasions. Some guys liked to just see them on the girls, so a girl might simply wear one around, while walking the patron on all fours on a dog leash.

Occasionally there were female patrons at The Chateau, always as submissives. Sir James, or his male assistant, personally dealt with the women clients. They handled regular weekly appointments for a fair number of women, Sir James told me.

Their clientele included the wealthy and prominent, and stars of entertainment, as well as the regular guys.

I spent many hours there, and persuaded the manager to allow me to observe some sessions. I saw one of the men wearing a studded dog collar, "walked" on all fours, on a leash. He barked when requested, sat when told, and begged when ordered.

I watched another man, among others, hand cuffed while spread eagle, hanging upside down, wearing nipple clips, and blind folded. The dominatrix called him every low-life name in the book and he wanted more. A cat o' nine tails was used on him, and it was obvious he loved it, as he climaxed during the episode. Nothing ever had contact with his penis.

While the Midwest place, at an earlier time, did many of the same things, the West Coast club did it a little fancier, a little flashier, and with a little more variations, including having the dominant men for submissive women. The Midwest club did not have any men working with the clientele.

My observations at these clubs helped me immensely when I had a call looking for different strokes. Plus, some of my own experiences helped as well. For example, there was the fellow, with whom I was acquainted, who was a toe-sucking fetishist. My very limited experiences with him taught me a lot about fetishists.

Some of my friends, especially in the erotic world, were knowledgeable about some of these unusual interests, and had over the years shared with me the details, which ultimately also helped me with calls that, perhaps, went further afield in subject matters than to which I was accustomed.

Many of the calls that were somewhat different were from people into latex and other fabrics. Some callers wanted to be verbally humiliated. Others wanted to be dominated throughout the entire call. Lots of guys loved to be restrained. Others wanted to be doing the restraining.

Of course, about the time I felt I had been called with every possible type of interest, I would be surprised by something new, and even more different.

However, with my visits to the bondage and discipline clubs, my own experiences, some of my friends' experiments with different sexual happenings, my own studying and reading, and research about various sexualities, I was able to work with any caller's fantasy that was ever presented to me. Of course, that meant as long as they were acceptable to Personal Services Club. There were subject matters I would never do, nor were even allowed by the fantasy phone sex club. I shared calls in this chapter that were of a different nature. Some were no doubt surprising, yet, some may not have been. In either case, they were all real fantasies of real people!

CHAPTER 5

TRIPS to PARADISE

Frequently, over the years, many people, including callers, would ask me about the various spots where I have had sex. Of course, I never found this question easy to answer because there have been so many places. Also, to me, an atmosphere can be more important than the actual location. However, to keep it simple, I usually would mention a couple of favorite places and that generally satisfied the curious.

In reality, I initially must travel back to my teenage years. Like most teenagers, during my youth, a car was the name of the sexual game. So much sex occurred in automobiles in my part of the country, (the Midwest), and I assume most parts, that it was a common occurrence, not a big deal. Now, if a guy and a girl got it on in a Corvette like someone and I did one time, that was more complicated, and brought us admiration from those in the know. Of course, drive-in theatres were one of the choice locations for parking and making out.

Parks were next on the list. Kansas City had lots of parks and I had my favorites. Sometimes, we would use a blanket on the grass in the parks, and gaze at the stars, for our romantic setting.

In my home or the boy's home were also places we used for intimate moments, when they were safely available. Again, there was not anything unusual about those areas.

However, while I was still in my teens, a boyfriend and I managed to do it in a piano shop where player pianos were being refurbished. Although we were clever enough not to get caught, it was not the most comfortable place for intimacies.

My sexual relationship with boats began in my teens and continued through adulthood. When I was a teenager, my family had a second home at Lake Lotawana, Missouri. We also had a pleasure boat. In fact, I had many friends with various kinds of boats. I quickly discovered I enjoyed sexual fun in any boat on the water. I have always wondered if that was how the inventor of the waterbed got the idea.

Continued on page 182

Rockin' Canoe

My calls were not limited to the United States, as the Canadians showed themselves to be plenty hot, as well, considering I routinely received calls from Canadians.

Since there was censorship regarding x-rated films and sexy reading material from the United States, the Canadians had to work a little harder to see my films and magazine spreads. When it came to their ideas on sex, they showed they were not slouches at their own brand of creativity, either.

One of those Canadians was Tommy, a professional skier, from Edmonton, Alberta, Canada. While visiting the States, he had seen one of my movies that showed my musical, oral abilities and he decided, then, that he needed to call me. He determined the perfect time was the day before he left to climb the Columbia Ice Field Glacier. After all, Tommy figured, his sex life would be non-existent while doing that.

Tommy's entire fantasy takes place in a canoe on a lovely summer day, on beautiful Lake Louise,

in Alberta, Canada. In his fantasy, the emphasis is on oral sex. He tells me how much he loves to go down on women, and that he loves to be sucked. He begins by going down on me, in the canoe, in the middle of the lake. This brings on his desire to fuck me. After that, he wants me to suck him. Tommy wants to breast-fuck me following my sucking. Finally, Tommy wants to "69," still in the canoe. This brings on the peak moment for Tommy.

Tommy's fantasy was typical of a lot of callers. He wanted to be in an unusual location, but, at the same time, wanted to enjoy a variety of sexual pleasures for both himself and his lover. As time progressed, I learned lots of callers are into unusual or different locations for their sexual fantasies.

* * * *

Sailboat Seduction

One summer evening I received a call from a thirty-one-year-old, named Bruno, a small business owner, who lived in Massachusetts. He described himself as having black hair, brown eyes, and a mustache. Bruno told me I had made an impression on him. He continued that he was a person who had something to say. That something was that he was crazy about me and wanted to meet me in person! Bruno said that he planned on having a party in my honor with great food, good drinks, nice people, if I would allow him to meet with me.

Bruno went on talking about how he wanted to be with me in July, and that we could do so much more in person than in phone sex. He felt I should give him an audition, he said. Finally, Bruno begins discussing his fantasy.

He wants us to be on a sailing boat, in a cove, with gentle waves slowly motioning the boat back and forth. We are sunbathing on the boat. I am wearing a neon orange bikini and he has on dark blue men's swimming trunks. He is lying next to me when I ask him to give me some suntan lotion. Bruno sits up and starts putting the lotion on my back, arms, legs, and thighs. He does this slowly and sensuously. He, then, turns me over and puts lotion on my shoulders and neck. He continues with my stomach and feet and legs. Bruno works his way along my upper inner thighs. Then, he goes back to my chest. This time, he reaches into my bikini top, with lotion on his hands, and begins massaging my breasts. He reaches behind me and unties my top and removes it. Bruno continues massaging my breasts, and starts licking and sucking them, too. He runs then, pulls off my bikini bottoms, as he continues his seduction.

After having completely removed my bikini, Bruno tongues my pussy, until he is sure I am very aroused. He raises my legs and rims me with his tongue, also.

When he is convinced I am really hot, he takes off his trunks, turns around and has me suck him while he continues eating me. When Bruno is convinced I climax, that sets him off. He quickly turns around and fucks me on top of the boat, missionary style, and climaxes in that position.

I found Bruno an exciting guy who enjoyed pleasing me. He was insistent that I orgasm in the fantasy phone call. Also, he occasionally mentioned the sway of the boat contributing to the hot action during the sex part of the call. That seemed to add to the excitement for Bruno. He still wanted to meet me, too, but, of course, I never did meet him. However, we did talk many times over the years.

* * * *

Sex On The Beach

I found a true southern gentleman in a caller named Tucker, a Nashville, Tennessee, native, living in North Carolina, near the ocean. Tucker was a really nice, fun guy, who had read and enjoyed an Interview I had had with Larry Flynt for **Hustler** magazine. Previously, he had talked with other erotic entertainers and film stars, such as Mai Lin and Candy Samples. In fact, he preferred to talk with females with whom he was familiar and already liked. Tucker and I chatted for a while about my connections to the South, by way of relatives and former boyfriends. It was easy to converse with this charmer.

Finally, Tucker told me his thoughts on women. He said he loved everything about a woman, including all her parts, from the sexy ones to the ordinary, and to the mind and intellect, as well. Tucker said he always could find something wonderful, sexy and (good) crazy in every woman.

Then, he told me his favorite sexual fun. Tucker enjoyed watching two women together and participating in threesomes with two women. However, his greatest sexual enjoyment came from oral sex. He said he loved it either way, both ways. He relished satisfying a woman and he delighted in being satisfied.

Tucker's phone fantasy sex begins with us on

a lovely North Carolina ocean beach, on a warm, clear night, close to his home. We have been walking along the beach sharing a bottle of wine. He stops to kiss me. We sit on the fine white sand and watch the waves, drink more wine, and continue kissing. Then, I unfasten his shorts and pull out his cock. I immediately go down on him. I use some of my fancier oral techniques on him. He orgasms this way.

After Tucker's orgasm, he told me how much he enjoyed the call. However, he felt badly he didn't get to reciprocate. I told him he could include that next time I talked to him. He enthusiastically agreed to my idea. Tucker came across as a sexy and charming guy, who loved romance mixed in with his sexual fantasies. Calls like his were always fun to have.

Continued from page 176

I also checked out, for some bedroom fun, one of the most beautiful hotels in the world, in Banff, Alberta, Canada, and thought that Signal Mountain made a beautiful backdrop.

Probably one of the most amazing places I ever had sex during that era, was in a hospital. Someone I was dating was a patient at the very hospital in which I was born. While visiting him, he had a bad case of raging hormones, and he was in such bad shape that I felt the need to take away his agony. Because he had on a full leg cast he needed to remain on his back, which was a good thing because I wanted to be able to move fast, if necessary. Luckily, I had on a dress that day.

Golf courses became a turn on for me beginning in my teens and were still a turn on as an adult. A couple of months after high school graduation, a guy I was dating and I ended up on the golf course at a country club on the other side of state line, in Kansas City, Kansas. We had his golf putter with us, on a full-moon night. After wandering around and doing a little putting, we ended up on the 18th hole. The summer night was perfect, the grass was thick and soft, and the foreplay was seductive. He showed me his ability to really get a hole in one. We had a great time. Afterward, he gave me a souvenir, too, the 18th hole pole and flag.

When he took me home late that night, I took the tall pole and flag into my family's home and left it leaning against the wall in our very formal dining room, and promptly went to bed. Our kind of golfing had been exhausting, after all.

The next morning, when my mother came through there on her way to fix breakfast, she was startled by this extremely strange sight. Then, when my father joined her, he also was somewhat curious about why there was this unusual apparition in the dining room.

When I finally got up that day, it had slipped my

mind that I had left my pole and 18th hole flag in the dining room. Plus, by the time I came downstairs it had moved to the kitchen. To say the least, I had to extemporaneously come up with a reasonable explanation for that being in our home. I'm sure it was a totally ridiculous effort, but it was accepted, and that pole and flag stayed in my parents' home for the next few years. It ended up in my bedroom next to my fireplace for my girlfriends to admire, and to remind me of a really hot evening, in a somewhat unusual spot, even though I had picked up a couple of mosquito bites as a reminder, too.

Actually, that wasn't my first golf course encounter, although it was my first pole and flag. Another time, when I was dating a young pro at a local country club to which my family belonged, he and I enjoyed a hot interlude on the course after hours one night. Only that time it was on the sixth hole.

My romance with, or on, golf courses occasionally continued over the next ten or fifteen years.

I enjoy golf, but I still can rarely look at a course without thinking about its potential for erotic games.

While I was a teenager, I also had a couple of occasions to enjoy a sexy moment on a tennis court, on a blanket, of course. It was an interesting place, but probably not one of my favorites.

Continued on page 192

B & D Oil Executive

An intriguing phone sex fantasy came from a caller named Teddy, who was an oil industry executive from Houston. On the phone, he came across as a sophisticated, worldly man, who found great pleasure in different kinds of erotica. As a result, Teddy felt uncomfortable sharing his desires at home or with friends.

Teddy's favorite sexual fantasies included watching Bondage and Discipline (also known as B and D) shows, movies, or performances, and his absolute favorite in that genre was watching women whipping women. He also liked to practice Domination when the occasional opportunity discreetly presented itself. Teddy's fantasies included being sucked while watching the B and D shows.

In the course of our conversation, Teddy told me he regularly went to live sex shows in Houston, and other cities. On this particular call, Teddy was into a certain show that really turned him on. He had seen it in Houston, on a bunch of occasions, including a few days before his call. This show had two Asian girls whipping a white girl. Then, the two Asian girls made love to the white girl. He said this was his very favorite live sex show. Teddy wanted us being present in the audience, at this show, included in his fantasy.

Teddy and I go to the live sex show where the three girls are performing. We are sitting in the audience watching the show, when he indicates he would like me to suck him. I kneel in front of him and unzip his trousers and pull them down exposing him. Then, I go down on him, while he continues watching the show and me, at the same time. I do this very briefly, when suddenly he interrupts my description to tell me he had climaxed.

As I had seen, and would continue to see, plenty of people have all kinds of different phone sex fantasies, that they feel the need to keep secret from those closest to them, but were happy and even relieved to expose to me. Teddy was no exception. When we ended the call he said he would be looking forward to talking to me again.

* * * *

The Dirty Baker

Sometimes, men call phone sex clubs to celebrate some special occasion or happening in their lives. Occasionally I received such calls. They were always special calls because these were usually celebratory moments for the callers.

One late evening, I received such a call from Brad, in St. Louis, who was celebrating his twenty-second birthday. I had talked with Brad before, so I generally knew what he was like, that he loved big tits, and that he was a nice guy.

This particular night, Brad wanted to chat for a while before doing anything sexy. Brad told me he was a baker and loved his career. He had spent a couple of years at MU, but his passion for the cooking industry took over. So, he quit college and learned to be a baker.

Since it was his birthday, he had been bar hopping before calling, he said. Brad told me he stopped on the way home and had his favorite breakfast – scrambled eggs and bacon. He had drunk champagne that night and danced to mellow rock music.

Then, he told me he loved to talk "dirty" to me. I knew it was time for his fantasy.

Brad comes to one of my live shows in San Francisco, in his fantasy. He gets turned on

watching it. I pay special attention to Brad, and flirt with him and tease him. After the show, I ask him to invite me out to breakfast, where he eats his favorite, of course.

Then, we go to his hotel suite, and I tell him to take off his clothes and to suck my breasts. After that, he goes down on me, requesting that I sit on his face. He wants me to stroke his cock while he is eating my pussy. He helps me stroke it, too.

Following that, he wants me to squat-fuck him, while facing him and, then, while facing away from him. Next, he wants me to suck him. For the finale, Brad asks me to lie on the bed while he fucks my tits and goes in and out of my mouth, at the same time. Brad climaxes doing this particular act. He requests that I cum with him in his fantasy.

Brad was having lots of fun that night. He was young, single, and very horny. He didn't feel comfortable picking up girls, and he didn't have a regular girlfriend, so he treated himself to something he truly enjoyed, talking to me. I was pleased I could give Brad a happy birthday treat.

* * * *

The Mile High Club

I received a call from Mike, one, hot summer evening. He was a FedEx pilot, based in Memphis, but was originally from the New Orleans area. Mike was both very soft-spoken, yet, quite talkative, too, about his job, and all the distant locations to where he'd traveled. He had previously seen my movies and stage shows in New York, and had tried to make contact with me for two years. Then, he found me through Personal Services Club. Personal Services said he would not talk to any house girls, but only to me.

Mike's phone fantasy begins with us taking off from Memphis on a flight to Paris. He is dressed in his uniform while I am naked sitting in the co-pilot's seat. We climb to about 30,000 feet and level off toward Paris. At that time, Mike starts playing with my breasts. The quarters are confining but he is able reach over and play with them, and I accommodate him the best that I can. I reach over and start stroking him through his pants. After about five minutes, he tells me it's time for automatic pilot.

First, he has me get up from my seat, and lie down in the aisle. Then, he leaves the pilot's seat and stands over me. He pulls his pants down, and he is rock hard. He motions me to sit up and suck him, which I do. Mike is very hot, so, he pushes me down and starts eating me. After I cum, he gets on top of me, and we starts fucking. It's very confining, but the excitement is overwhelming for him, so, he cums, and, then, just collapses on me. His first comment is, " Welcome to the mile high club," as he pulls up his pants, goes to the pilot's seat, and resumes flying the plane.

Mike went on to tell me it got very lonely sometimes up at 30,000 feet and his mind would wander to sexual activities. I didn't think Mike particularly liked his real co- pilot.

I was glad I was able to fulfill Mike's fantasy. It was pretty basic, but very exciting. As a member of the Mile High Club I knew, first hand, the sexual excitement 30,000 feet above the clouds can be. Mike did not call, again, but I would have flown with him anytime.

* * * *

California Beachhead

Early one evening, Thomas, from the Detroit area, called. Thomas sounded charming, sexy, and very nice. Initially, he wanted to chat about various subjects, not involving sexual matters. He talked about his career as an executive in the auto industry, and about his parents' home near Ft. Meyers, Florida. Further, Thomas mentioned his visits to some of the better-known national and state parks. Also, he told me he liked my movies.

Thomas described himself as a non-drinker, who was both a reformed alcoholic, and a former smoker. He told me he had very dark hair, piercing black-brown eyes, and was 5 feet 10 inches, with a decent body. Continuing, he referred to himself as an Everything Man, but mostly a leg man. He loved women's legs, and adored Juliet Prowse, who had the all-time perfect legs, he thought.

Then, Thomas got to the primary subject for which he called, his fantasy.

Thomas has us spending a beautiful sunshiny, clear day on a California nude beach. After arriving there, I take off my hot pink bikini and he removes his azure blue trunks. We go playing in the surf, and that's when we notice all the naked hot babes and guys, on the fine, white, sandy beach.

After some of this fun in the sun and surf, we go to our blanket. We are aware that there are sexual activities going on around us. Thomas gets aroused and asks me for a "head job," as he calls it. First, though, he desires to massage my legs and run his hands up and down my calves and thighs. I hear him getting more turned on as we talk about him handling my legs.

Now, Thomas is ready for his head job. He lies back on the blanket, on the beach, and I give him a lengthy, detailed, very hot sucking. He loves every second of it. At one point, I rub my breasts on his penis and, then, go back to sucking him off. Suddenly, Thomas has a mighty orgasm. The phone practically smokes.

I found some of Thomas' fantasy fairly common. Lots of men, it seemed, liked pretty, sandy shores, for the backgrounds of their fantasies, although most men never thought to make their beach, a nude beach. However, Thomas had visited a nude beach before, and he was crazy about it, and had wanted oral sex there, in his mind, ever since. It was fun to have given him a taste of his long-time fantasy, and I could tell the term "beachhead" had a whole new meaning to him when we said our goodbyes.

Continued from page 184

When I was sixteen, I acquired a taste for lovemaking on beaches. The first time I actually thought about it was at a then-popular swimming lake in the Kansas City area, called Kernodles. I had met a very sexy guy with whom I envisioned making love there. Although we did not make love at that lake, I think that is when my eternal romance with beaches started. Oh, yes, I did make wonderful, torrid love with this very sexy fellow, who really turned me on, but it was in private, in his bed. It may not have been an unusual place, but it was the beach at the lake when I discovered how much I wanted him. This is an example of atmosphere being more important than location, when a person really wants to make love with someone really special.

During my teenage years, I managed to do intimate things on beaches from Florida to California and back again, as well as in the Midwest.

Beaches still are a romantic, sensual place to me, and I have had my sexy moments with them as an adult, also.

I found swimming pools and jacuzzis were always fun for a little sex play, too. I tried them out in my teens and continued those locations through adulthood.

In my teens, my family and I visited New York City, for a convention. In the course of our time in the city, I met a seductive male who introduced me to sex, New York style. We had a steamy adventure in his car in Central Park.

My boyfriend and I, during our college days, were attending his fraternity's annual Purple Passion Party, and somehow we ended up on the roof of the building, in which the party was being held, and there we decided to have a personal, sexual moment. It was exciting on the roof, but for one thing. His fraternity had rented the place for the party in a not-so-good area of the city. So, while we were doing it we were being serenaded by the constant sound of police sirens.

During Spring Break, he and I stepped back into time and had sex in a famous, very old, and elegant, small hotel in the heart of the French Quarter, in New Orleans. The rooms were full of antiques and the décor was of previous centuries. I felt a little like Scarlett O'Hara, having sex in that location.

Through rest of my college years, and as an adult, I managed to find all kinds of places to enjoy sexual, sensual pleasure in some form or other.

When I was still at the University, a free-spirited fellow student and I decided we were hot for each other, and we made excellent use of the leather couch in a dean's office. We used to joke how we "fucked" the school. That was exciting, but I hate to think back what would have happened if we had gotten caught, especially since we were both so close to graduation.

Of course, there were the mundane places like friends' and students' apartments and homes, and my own place too. However, that doesn't mean there was anything routine about the sex!

Hayrides were extremely popular in my area of the country. Taking kegs of beer on the rides were virtually mandatory. I discovered that those rides could turn erotic after drinking some beer, and bouncing around, with a hot boyfriend. I enjoyed that sex but it has its drawbacks. Hay gets everywhere, and I mean everywhere, when having sex on hayrides.

As a young adult, I dated a fellow who was really into the sound of rain, to the point that when we made love he would turn on a faucet or shower as background noise. We used to go to his lake place and turn on the fake rain. Naturally, he was into shower sex. During rainy weather, he was pretty much a walking erection. I found him fascinating because he took something that seems to turn on a lot of people and turned it into a hot obsession. I used to hope for rain a lot while I was dating him.

Sometimes, it would get very interesting with him during the rainy season. One time, it was pouring and he drove us to a top of a bluff, where there is a famous statue, called The Scout, overlooking Kansas City. We got naked in the car, and, then, dashed out into the pouring rain, and made soaking-wet love up against that statue. I was glad it was a warm rain!

Continued on page 202

Lonesome in New York

Late one evening, about midnight, I received a call from Larry, of New York City. Larry's wife was visiting Vermont, and he was feeling lonesome. I had previously talked to Larry on several occasions, so I knew quite a bit about him. He was the head of a large company, and a workaholic. Also, his wife frequently traveled. With these factors combined, Larry's sex life was at low ebb. He loved sex, he claimed, but rarely had the time or opportunity.

On this occasion, Larry had run into some close friends of mine, (erotic film stars Samantha Fox and Bobby Astyr), earlier in the evening, at a local midtown restaurant. Then, while still out, he saw Kelli Nichols, another lady, who had starred in erotic films. Just seeing these people, in person, was almost too much for Larry. He came home, ran to the phone, and arranged a call with me.

First, though, this time when he called, Larry was anxious to fly to the West Coast to meet me. He wanted to catch a plane the very next day. I had to convince Larry to settle down and to not do that.

When that was resolved, Larry was ready for his fantasy.

In his fantasy, Larry flies to California and gets together with me. We take a blanket to a lovely

Southern California beach. Larry and I go into the ocean and play in the water. He removes my bikini in the water. I remove his trunks. Then, we head for our blanket, which is spread out on the sand.

Larry kisses me with soft wet kisses, and he fondles my bare breasts. Then, he lies back on the blanket and pushes my face toward his hard cock. He asks me to kneel over him, and to suck him, among other things. I lick him and suck him, while on my knees, and I play with, and squeeze, his ass, just the way he wishes it. Larry requests that I keep sucking him and that I do some of my fancier techniques. I comply with Larry's desires.

Now, Larry tells me he wants to cum orally, and he wants to hold my head down, in his phone sex fantasy, when he cums. He asks me to describe it, which I do. This sets Larry off, and suddenly, he cums very hard.

Larry was so pleased and relaxed after he came, I could almost visualize his ear-to-ear grin through the phone. We conversed a little longer about erotica, but we kept it very brief. Larry was about to fall asleep. I knew he would have nice dreams that night.

* * * *

Jamaica Jamboree

One winter morning, I received a call from Allen, who lived in Ottawa, Ontario, Canada. Allen said it was ten below zero, in Ottawa, at the time he called. He said it was so cold he wanted me to help warm him up. He was funny and sweet, and a little nervous. Allen told me this was his first call for fantasy phone sex.

Since he had to take the day off from work because of the weather, and, as a result, he was both cold and housebound, he decided to call me, and see what phone sex was like. He said he had fantasized about me since seeing me in a magazine a few months back.

Allen described himself as twenty-three years old, 5 feet 6 inches, with brown hair and brown eyes. He said he loved to drink Tom Collins, and that he was a tit man. Allen said he definitely loved tits! They were his number one turn on.

Finally, he got around to talking about his fantasy. Since it was a cold and snowy winter in so many places, I wasn't surprised at its location. Like so many others at that time of the year, as I had previously discovered, his fantasy took place in a lovely, warm setting.

Allen's fantasy takes place in Jamaica. We are on a snow white, sandy beach, lying on a

blanket, and drinking a jug of Tom Collins. I take off my royal blue bikini and his green swimsuit. We kiss, and I rub my breasts against his chest. Then, I start working my way down him, kissing and licking his chest, first. I continue licking him all over as I move further down his body. When I reach his cock, I suck him. Allen requests that I talk about doing a hard suck on him. He pulls on my legs to turn my body more toward him, so that he can finger me while I continue the oral sex.

Next, Allen makes it known he wants to fuck me. Initially, he wants me on top, so he can play with, and suck, my breasts. He asks me to fuck him hard, with a lot of action, in his fantasy. After some of this, Allen rolls us over, staying inside me. He raises my legs and brings them up high toward my chest and he rams me, fucking me with hard, long, deep strokes. Suddenly, Allen lets out a yell, as he enthusiastically cums.

Afterward, Allen told me he felt a whole lot hotter than he did before the call. He, also, said he had cum so hard he felt drained and was thinking about taking a late morning nap. Allen said he felt wonderful, and that I was an incredible woman. He finished the call by telling me he would love to talk to me again.

* * * *

Dinner at the Falls

Men were hot in Buffalo, New York, as I found out one cold winter night, when I received a call from Oliver. Previously, he had read about me in **Screw** magazine, and in **Hustler,** as well as in other various publications. Oliver was an aficionado of erotica and a collector of erotic films and photos, including some of my own movies and photos.

It was obvious he was very proud of his collections, which included some of my films, like **S.O.S.,** and **Devil Inside Her**, as well as other erotic hits, such as, **Debbie Does Dallas**, and **Barbara Broadcast**. Oliver, also, talked about his favorite photos in his collection of hundreds, which included Merle Michaels, Laurie Smith, and me.

Besides collecting erotica, Oliver was fascinated with "swinging." He discussed Plato's Retreat, in New York City, and their schedules for couples and singles. He never actually said whether he had swung or not, but he did ask for all pertinent information regarding going to Plato's Retreat.

Then, Oliver was ready for his fantasy phone sex. He told me he was very horny and wanted to feel really great. So, he already had a scenario in mind.

Oliver has us in a motel by Niagara Falls, close enough we can see and hear the falls from our room. I am naked and dozing, when I suddenly

am awakened by my legs being spread apart, and the feeling of a hot, wet tongue in my pussy. Oliver tells me how delicious I taste as he turns me on with his lips and tongue, in his fantasy. Now, he turns around, and we "69." He requests I stop sucking him for a brief period and stroke him with my hand. He asks me to describe my hand action in detail. Then, Oliver requests I spend a lot of time feeling, touching, and gently squeezing his testicles. After some of this, Oliver wants me to go back to sucking. This is when he explodes in ecstasy.

Following his moments of ecstasy, Oliver told me how much he genuinely enjoyed looking at spread shots of women. He said he was totally a pussy man. In addition to looking, he loved practicing cunnilingus on women. He explained when he got women off that way, it would sometimes cause him to have orgasms. He finished our conversation by telling me he took great pleasure in making women cum. As we were hanging up, I thought to myself, there must be a lot of happy women in the Buffalo area.

One special boyfriend and I, (before my career in erotica), used to have sex at all kinds of places including his downtown offices and his south town office. He was pretty adventurous and was always looking for new places for us.

One of the most fascinating places I ever made love was in an airplane, when I became a member of the Mile High Club. Al and I and another couple were flying up to Minneapolis, on business, one clear night in a 10-seater Cessna. Somewhere along the way, Al decided I should become a member of the Mile High Club. I thought it was a great idea! We left the flying to his co-pilot and he and I enjoyed ourselves throughout the entire plane. I discovered I loved having sex in an airplane! It was a wonderful feeling.

Over the years I would have calls from men, and receive fan mail from men, who fantasized having me in my dressing room. Well, on rare occasions, I did have sex in one of my dressing rooms. Generally, I did not, though, because I wanted to save my energy, sexual and otherwise, for stage.

From my all-time favorite list of places comes a simple one. It was on a bearskin rug, in front of an oversized wood-burning fireplace, with a crackling fire, on a cold winter night, in my own home! Sexy music in the background was a prerequisite. With a wonderful lover it could last for hours.

There are so many places I could talk about making love and having sex that I did check out over the years, but this gives a general idea of some of my hot spots. Of course, I still have some fantasy locations I have not yet tried. However, I am keeping them in mind for the future.

My callers frequently cared a great deal about the locations of their erotic fantasies. While some, of course, were perfectly content with any bedroom or living room; others were specific about shapes of beds, and sizes of beds. Even the kinds of fabrics and color scheme of the surroundings were important factors to certain callers.

However, many callers had places in mind where they wanted their fantasies to occur. Hotels were often mentioned, and the callers' offices were very popular places. Some callers were turned on by the idea of sex inside movie theaters. In or around swimming pools were popular.

Continued on page 212

Cinema Delight

I received a call from Larry, on a cloudy March afternoon, from Silver Springs, Maryland. Larry wanted to make the clouds go away, at least, for him, so he decided to give me a call. Since Larry and I had already conversed a week earlier, he knew he enjoyed talking to me. Larry told me he was tall, with curly brown hair and green eyes, and that he was a government contractor. His free time was limited, because of his career, so he didn't have a lot of chances to think sexy. So, when the opportunity arose that afternoon, he grabbed it.

Larry had seen movies of mine and really liked them. He especially was fond of one in particular, and he wanted to watch that movie in a theatre with me. That's not all Larry wanted in his fantasy. He also wanted me to go down on him while watching the movie, and for me to imitate myself. In fact, Larry wanted a "different, far out, wild blow job."

In his phone sex fantasy, Larry and I are in an adult theatre, sitting discreetly near the back. My movie comes on and we watch the action. Larry unzips his pants and pulls his cock out. He's just about ready for his own exploits. He requests I go down on him in the same way as what's showing on the screen, while we're watching it.

I start sucking Larry, as he continues viewing the movie. I emulate what's happening on the screen and Larry gets extremely excited. He reaches the point where he is ready to cum. Larry wants to do it like it's done in the movie. He requests I open my mouth and pull slightly away from his cock. Then, he "shoots" his cum into my mouth, while watching the similar scene on the screen, at the same time. Larry sounds like he has a terrific orgasm.

Afterward, Larry told me the sun was shining, over his space, anyway. He was happy and relaxed, for sure. He thanked me for this call and, again, for the previous call. Larry was full of praise as he told me how much he liked talking to me. I knew I would be hearing from him again soon.

* * * *

Stressful Trial Attorney

Terry, from Evanston, Illinois, called me on a cold March morning, ready and wanting to get rid of his stress before leaving for the office. He was a trial attorney, in his mid-thirties, who had a date with the courtroom that morning. Terry described himself as 6 feet, and having dark-brown, wavy hair and azure blue eyes. Women said he was good looking, he mentioned, sounding a little embarrassed.

A vacation in the Bahamas was coming up in Terry's life in about three weeks. He told me he needed to get away from the intense pressure induced by his career. He was ready to play on the beaches, gamble in the casinos, and chase beautiful women. However, this specific morning, he wanted a sneak preview of his upcoming vacation.

Initially, Terry said he was a little of "everything" man, when it came to women, but, then, admitted he was mostly a lover of big tits and women's asses.

Terry's fantasy begins with the two of us together in the Bahamas. We decide to go to the beach, after gambling all morning. The hotel has put together a picnic lunch and a bottle of wine for us. They manage to come up with a blanket, too.

We arrive at the beach and pick out a lovely, isolated location. Next we decide to take a swim in the clear blue water. While swimming, Terry comes over and removes the top of my black bikini and plays with my breasts and sucks my nipples, right there in the Caribbean.

After a taste of my breasts, Terry is ready for more. So, we get out of the water and move to our blanket. Terry removes his swim trunks and pulls off my bikini bottoms. He lies back on the blanket. I start by sucking his nipples and I slowly work my way down him, licking his chest and stomach as I go. Finally, when I reach his cock, I suck him. Then, we "69."

Following that action, Terry has us fuck with me on top, so that he can suck my breasts, at the same time. Then, he has us reverse positions, putting him on top. I wrap my legs around his neck. At this point, Terry is so hot he is ready to explode. He cums hard on my face and breasts, his places of choice.

In Terry's fantasy, after his orgasm, we lie

together on the blanket briefly. Then, we share our wine and lunch in this romantic setting.

Terry was definitely feeling better by the end of our call. He was ready to take on the courtroom that day with a smile. I figured he would also be smiling when he got to those pretty Bahamian beaches. I knew I would be hearing from Terry again.

* * * *

Fargo Body Builder

Shane, a North Dakotan, called me one evening from Fargo, North Dakota, feeling very sexual. He described himself as 5 feet 11 inches, with dishwater blonde hair and hazel eyes. Shane said he had a decent body and was an all-round amateur athlete. Professionally, he was a bodybuilder.

That night, Shane had been watching some erotic films at home and found himself ready to do more than watch. So, he decided to talk to me.

In the beginning of our conversation, Shane said he was primarily a tit man. He loved everything about them, but especially sucking and fucking them.

He preferred big tits, so that he could have them squeezed around his cock. Of course, that wasn't all that Shane liked. He also said oral sex, either way, was wonderful, but he especially loved to eat pussy. It was obvious Shane was ready for his fantasy.

Shane's fantasy takes place in Cancun, Mexico, one of his favorite spots in the world. Although he doesn't drink, he wants us to start out at a nightclub called Carlos O'Brien's. Shane enjoys the action there. He likes the girls rubbing their boobs on people when they drink shots of rum. So, Shane orders me a shot and the girls rub their tits on both of us. He loves the girls' boob action so much he decides it's time for us to go somewhere more intimate.

We arrive at our villa and instantly end up in the bedroom, where Shane undresses me. Immediately, Shane kisses my breasts and sucks them. Then, he travels quickly down to my pussy, where he plants more kisses. He gently nibbles and tongues me there. After some of that, he lies back on the bed, and he grabs my breasts hanging down in his face, and sucks my hard nipples. Following this action, I lick him all the way down to his cock. At that point, I suck Shane. Now, he puts his cock between my breasts, in his fantasy, and I rub his cock with them and lick the head between the rubs. Then, we "69."

Finally, Shane has me lie back on the bed. He straddles my chest and tit-fucks me, holding my breasts together around his cock. As he strokes my breasts, I lick the head with each thrust. Next, he moves further up on me and "fucks" my mouth. Suddenly, he pulls out and cums hard on my breasts.

Shane was ecstatic and thrilled about the whole experience, after his orgasm. He loved his fantasy phone call and he hoped to have more conversations with me in the future. I was looking forward to hearing from this sweet, courteous guy again.

* * * *

Memories from Rio

Occasionally a call would come from a man who wanted to relive some special moment in his life. He loved an earlier, wonderful experience, and by means of a phone sex fantasy it was brought back to life for him. A call of this kind was generally really nice to do because the caller ended up feeling happy, as well as good, by the end of the call.

Randy, of Galveston, Texas, called one night with memories he wanted to briefly enjoy again. First, however, he wanted to chat about other things, including my films that he had seen. He spoke of his favorite scenes, and how much he genuinely liked my movies.

After we discussed my movies, Randy decided to describe himself. He stated he was short, hairy all over, with brown hair and brown eyes, and that he was an old Chuck Berry and Elvis Presley fan. Randy also said he was primarily an ass man, but liked it all. He loved to eat pussy and to lick ladies' butts.

Randy had another thing to tell me before his phone fantasy. He absolutely did not like what he referred to as "Yankee accents." He did not like actors, including erotic actors and actresses, who spoke with Yankee accents. However, he loved what he thought was my southern way of speaking. Randy said he got turned on just listening to me talk about anything. He also loved my name, which he called "Southern," too.

Finally, Randy was ready for his fantasy, which was based on what he referred to as a highlight of his life. During his Navy days, he somehow had a brief, but highly memorable experience in Rio de Janeiro, Brazil. Randy had made love with a beautiful Hungarian girl on Copacabana Beach, which was something he would never forget. Now, Randy wanted to make love with me on the beach in Galveston.

Randy's fantasy begins with the two of us walking along the beach holding hands. He's also carrying a bag. There is a full moon lighting up our way, a warm gentle breeze is blowing the palm trees, and we can hear and see the pounding surf. We stop in a fairly secluded area

of the beach, and he lays out a blanket he was carrying in the bag. We sit on the blanket and he opens a bottle of wine and pours it into 2 glasses he also gets from the bag.

Randy has on khaki shorts and a shirt. I have on a blue sundress, with nothing on underneath it. We drink our wine and make small talk.

Then, Randy leans over and gently kisses me. I respond, and the kissing becomes more intense, more passionate. He takes off his shirt and I rub his chest, playing with his nipples, kissing and sucking them. I lick his entire chest, and I unfasten his shorts and pull them down. He unbuttons the top of my dress and exposes my breasts. He gently kneads them, and plays with them. Randy sucks my nipples, while I stroke his cock with my hand.

Randy sensuously pushes me down and raises my skirt, exposing my pussy. He spreads my legs apart and begins eagerly eating and licking my entire pussy area. Randy raises my legs high in the air and rims me. While doing this he turns around, offering me his cock to suck. I suck him slowly, at first, and pick up speed, while he's enjoying my holes with his mouth and tongue.

Now, Randy wants to fuck me. He has me get on top of him and straddle his cock. I sit on it very slowly, initially, so he can get the full feeling of entering my pussy. Then, I go up and down on him rhythmically. He turns me over, when he's close to cumming. He fucks me hard and deep, with him on top, until he yells in delight as he cums, and I cum with him, in his fantasy.

As soon as he finishes cumming, he asks me to suck him some more, which I immediately do. Suddenly, Randy is yelling again, as he cums a second time!

When Randy's phone sex fantasy was completed, Randy was one very relaxed guy. He had had two orgasms, and had gotten to fulfill a fantasy of his wonderful memory.

It was great to make Randy feel so good and help him relive a fantastic moment in his life. He was very happy and completely satisfied, he said.

I was thrilled for Randy, and pleased about the way he felt afterward. I really enjoyed his call, and I hoped I would get to talk with Randy again.

Continued from page 203

Lots of callers wanted to have their fun in the shower. More than a few wanted fantasy sex on stage, in an adult show, or even in an x-rated film. One caller desired his fantasy sex at his wife's boyfriend's home!

The most popular location outside the bedroom, though, hands down, was on a beach. Beach fantasies were so popular that I could have several callers in a row who requested that location. The beaches were everywhere, in the states, and all over the world. While there were often similarities in the kind of sex in the beach fantasies, there were plenty of differences, too. Most of the time, those callers wanted romance and wine, but not always. Sometimes, the callers simply wanted to relive a memory or moment from their past, which happened to be connected to a beach.

The calls I shared in this chapter placed a lot of emphasis on the importance of the location for the fantasies; yet, these were only a handful of the huge number of calls I received that stressed favored, fantasy hot spots.

CHAPTER 6

BON APPÉTIT

Some of my most popular and frequent calls involved oral sex fantasies or desires for "how-to" lessons. There were even callers who only wanted to discuss my oral abilities or their own past experiences. Occasionally I would have a call from someone who would have his lady present on the phone, so I could give her instructions in the art of cocksucking. At times, I had calls where I would literally direct the woman on what to do as she did it. Those particular ones made for intriguing calls since I could not actually see what was happening. I had to depend on him or her to describe the action that I directed.

Generally, if people other than my fans called Personal Services, and requested to talk to a star, who excelled in the area of oral sex, those calls would be directed to me. That was something in the field of erotica for which I was noted throughout the world, by way of my films, my columns and writings, interviews, reviews, layouts, and other media, as well.

Continued on page 226

Oral Fixation

Sometimes, a screener would call me when I was not scheduled to have calls, asking me if there was any chance I could please take a call, anyway. The screener would always be apologetic and would never attempt to pressure me to have an off-schedule call. The reason she would call is because she had a request from a fan of mine, who wished to talk with me, at that very moment, and had convinced her that he could not call back later. Depending on my availability, at the time, I would say yes or no.

On a certain spring afternoon, I received a call from Mary, a screener, asking if I could please take said okay, and she gave me the information about this fan, whom I immediately contacted.

The impatient fan, Hayes, from Denver, who couldn't wait to talk to me, was so pleased when he heard my voice on the phone, that he began the conversation thanking me over and over again for having this untimely call with him

Hayes told me he was thirty years old, and a large bookstore manager in the greater Denver area. He simply described himself as good looking and a lover of sex. In fact, he added, he was bisexual. He loved women, especially going down on them; he loved men, especially sucking them. It dawned on me that Hayes might have a little bit of an oral fixation, although Hayes did add he loved to be called nasty names, too.

Hayes finally mentioned why he had such an immediate need to talk to me. He wanted to discuss oral sex, meaning, in this instance, sucking men! He told me he preferred long, thin cocks, and that he wasn't too sure what to do with thick, bulging ones. Hayes asked me for suggestions to make his sucking abilities better and more versatile. He wanted to add some "specialties" to his style, too. While he enthusiastically approached it, he felt his techniques could use some improvement. Hayes had plans that evening that included oral sex with some guy, and he wanted it to be the best it could be. He wanted to impress this fellow, who had a beautiful, large, straight penis, according to him, but he had not yet had his lips on it.

We spent the entire call discussing the pros and cons of different ways to improve his sucking abilities. Hayes really wanted to gain knowledge on this subject, and was uninterested in being turned on during this call.

For the last minute or so, of the call, Hayes reiterated his love of going down on women, as well. However, he said he thought he had his style perfected in that area. Following that comment, I wished him success in his cocksucking endeavors, and said good-bye.

While Hayes was not my typical caller, I did receive a certain percentage of calls of a similar vein. My oral abilities seemed to have intrigued people from all over the world, as I had discovered over the years. So, I wasn't particularly surprised by Hayes' desire to discuss oral sex techniques on men with me. I hoped he found our conversation beneficial, and that he was happy with the ultimate results.

* * * *

"Greek" and "Head"

Tommy from Paducah, Kentucky, called one evening, feeling very happy and exceptionally horny. He had previously conversed with a couple of house girls, but, tonight, Tommy wanted to talk to an erotic film star, me. He immediately told me he was into "Greek" and "Head," and that he was a tit man, first, and an ass man, second. He went on to say that he fantasized about oral sex all the time, but had not had any in over a year. His life had been going through some changes.

He, also, talked about his fantasies regarding anal sex. Tommy said that although he had participated in anal sex several times, that he still fantasized about doing it almost as much as oral sex. The main reason he thought he fantasized about it so much was that his partners were rarely able to "accommodate" him, he claimed. Tommy added that his penis was a "nice, wide, straight, almost 9 inches."

Fantasies were important to him, Tommy continued, because he was really strait-laced. As a result, his fantasies were to the point, without any embellishments. He would simply get it on with the female and get off, as he put it.

Tommy's phone sex fantasy is he wants to be sucked in bed. Tommy is lying in bed and I walk in. He reaches for me and kisses me. Then, I unzip his pants, and remove them from him. I take off his underwear. He kisses me again and pulls my sheer red top off me. After he briefly fondles my breasts, Tommy pushes me down toward his bare, throbbing cock. I immediately start sucking him. I continue doing this until he has an orgasm.

After the fantasy sex part of the call was completed, Tommy told me that he would love to do it the Greek way, next time.

Since phone sex between strangers is all about fantasies, it seemed logical that Tommy would make phone sex calls to enjoy his special fantasies. Tommy definitely felt his fantasy had been fulfilled by the time we said goodbye.

* * * *

Lick Them Clean

A call came late one evening, from Earl, an insurance executive, in snowy Hartford, Connecticut. He said he'd been to a banquet that evening and now was home and wanted a hot, erotic film star, meaning me, in his king-sized, heated waterbed.

Earl described himself as 5 feet 11 inches, 200 pounds, with blue eyes and brown hair. He told me he loved big tits and lots of oral sex.

This particular night, Earl says he wants plenty of sex in his fantasy, and he knows exactly what he wants us to do. He has me begin by licking his whole body, which gives him goose bumps, he

says. Then, Earl has me suck his cock. Following that, Earl fucks me with me on top, and he sucks my breasts, at the same time.

Earl is very hot, but he has more fantasy sex in mind. He asks me to suck him again and to play with his bottom, too. Now, I can tell Earl is sizzling. However, he has a couple of more things left to complete his fantasy.

This is the point when Earl practically begs me to play with my breasts, while he watches. Then, he desires for me to suck my own nipples. I verbally describe these actions to him. Before long, Earl requests cumming on my tits, and he tells me he wishes for me to offer them to him, so, that he may lick them clean, afterward. The result is Earl has a huge orgasm.

I had fulfilled Earl's phone sex fantasy quite well. He, ecstatically, told me I had been a fantasy figure for a long time, since he had seen my first movie. Never in his wildest imagination did he dream he would even have phone fantasy sex with me. I knew when the call ended that Earl would be dreaming about this call for a long time.

* * * *

Jody's Challenge

At 12:30 A.M., one April morning, I answered the phone to a Personal Services' screener, who had a call for me, and also wanted to give me a heads up about the caller.

She told me she had attempted to discourage this man from talking to me, especially at that late hour, because he had a "history" with Personal Services. However, he was insistent on speaking with me. So, here she was, on the phone, giving me information about the caller. The screener apologized, but I told her that was unnecessary whatever the situation was. I was curious though, and was wishing she would get to the problem.

Before the screener told me about it, she gave me all other pertinent information regarding the man. Finally, she shared what had gotten her all worked up. Jack, an engineer with GM, near the Detroit area, had talked to many house girls and three other stars, previously. They unanimously reported the same thing – Jack was almost impossible to get off! She reported that they said if he did climax it took a longtime and constant heavy sexual talk for him to get there. He frequently did not orgasm, but insisted the girls keep trying until they were darn near hoarse. Strangely enough, though, she added, that the girls liked him for his enthusiasm. They just hated trying to make him cum. Sometimes, he would talk to two house girls at the same time, for a fantasy threesome, but it was still just as hard to get him off. Plus, to make matters worse, she thought he had been drinking that night.

By this time, I was totally awake, and was absolutely thrilled about my middle of the night caller. Well, I thought to myself, I think I'll stay away from much small talk if he is interested in a sex fantasy.

It was time to talk to Jack, who was around forty years old. Initially, Jack did chat briefly with me. He wanted to discuss the weather, and his drinking habits. He said he routinely drank too much and had been drinking wine all that evening. I wondered if that was the case every time he had a call. Now, it was sexy fantasy time.

We drink wine as Jack plays some hot music. He nuzzles and kisses me all over. He asks me to lick his chest and his body, which I do. Now, I verbally suck his cock in great detail, followed by some "69ing."

After the head-to-head oral sex, we fuck, with me on top, then, doggie style, and, next, missionary position with my legs around his neck. Jack is obviously turned on, and he's breathing hard, but he isn't there yet.

Jack requests I suck him, again, in his phone fantasy. I describe a blistering hot oral sex scene. Suddenly, Jack lets out a scream at the top of his lungs, and I think success! However, I was a little premature patting myself on the back.

I comment on his cumming nicely, while he's still sounding a little wild. Somehow, he manages to tell me, he hasn't cum yet. I am amazed, but don't have a chance to really think about it because he wishes to fuck me some more, missionary style, again. We go for it, and, then, he's screaming even louder than before. I am hoping none of his neighbors hear his blood-curdling scream! This time I am afraid to comment on cumming, but he finally winds down and sputters that he came.

Following Jack's orgasm, he briefly complimented and thanked me before saying goodnight. He imagined he would sleep well that night, he stated, as he said his good byes.

The fact Jack had had a nice orgasm, or any kind of orgasm, for that matter, caused me to have a mental sigh of relief. Since I had been somewhat prepared by the screener, I had gone for strong steamy stuff, right away. However, it seemed Jack would come to the edge but had a tremendous amount of trouble crossing over. He did cross over though, eventually, with an orchestra of trumpets blasting their sounds.

* * * *

World Traveler

    Sam, from Flagstaff, Arizona, called one evening, wanting to visit with me as well as have fantasy phone sex. He told me he was a transplanted native Missourian, who moved away from there when he was about twenty years old. He attended the University of Kansas, and, for many years, was involved with a M.U. girl, whom he almost married.
    He discussed his career as a pilot, and, eventually, as a charter flight service owner. Sam had traveled the world many times over, during his careers. In fact, the night he called me, he was going to be heading to Texas, after we hung up. Through his travels, he had fallen in love with the Pacific Islands, and was soon moving to one of them for about a year. Following that, Sam planned to spend the rest of his life living in southwest Africa, his most favorite area in the world. He was going to run his business from there, too.
    As Sam got closer to his sex fantasy, he described his cock to me, somewhat sheepishly yet proudly, too, telling me it was about 12 inches long, very straight, and circumcised. He began talking about my movies, also. He had seen a couple of them that really turned him on.

    Finally, Sam mentions his fantasy. He wants me to suck him, and he wants me to talk about certain hot scenes of mine from some of my

movies, at the same time. I fulfill this request, and while I am doing this, (talking about sucking him, specifically, at the moment), he interrupts me to discuss my hometown in Missouri, filming, and me.

He started asking me questions again about my life before erotica. It was somewhat unusual to change gears so abruptly, but if that was what Sam wanted to talk about, then, it was fine with me. He sounded relaxed and pleasant, but he never went back to the fantasy that night.

Continued from page 216

When I agreed to make my first erotic film, **Portrait,** for Gerard Damiano, he asked me as a legitimate actress to star in the movie. However, he also inquired if I had any special talents of a sensual nature. Much to his surprise I said that I did have a few things for which I was noted in my private life, but one was really something extraordinary.

I had already discovered that Jerry (Damiano) had a great sense of humor, so I figured he would be both amused and intrigued by my special talent. I was correct.

I told Jerry I could sing songs, lyrics and all, (not humming), while sucking. After he got over his astonishment, he asked me how that affected a man, and the history behind it.

The effect on a man was always phenomenal, when I had chosen to share my talent. The reaction was generally the same, the man would be laughing from the waist up, and loving it from the waist down as he fought to keep from cumming. That kind of response had been 100%.

Of course, I told Damiano I could do many oral things, including other creations of mine, but I really loved the singing and sucking. I figured I was simply a frustrated singer at heart, who loved oral sex.

As for the history of the birth of The Singing Cocksucker, it began during my swinging days, when I was going with John. One year, during the holidays, he and I had been out partying with our favorite regular couple.

When we had gotten home to my place, the four of us decided to enjoy the swinging moment, and to drink some more bubbly.

I was filled with holiday spirit, and for reasons unknown to me, while practicing my talents on John, I burst into a popular holiday tune, "Jingle Bells." I began the song with its first verse, the words clearly understood. He was startled, amazed, and laughing, but the reaction was totally positive. By the time I got to the chorus, he was holding on for dear life. I barely got the song finished.

The other couple watched, of course, and loved it. The husband asked if I would honor him with a song.

So, keeping the holiday spirit alive, I did it again. The reaction and results were exactly the same.

Afterward, I asked them about it, and they found it hard to explain how they could be laughing and so turned on at the same time. However, John and the other friend asked me to please keep it up. The wife loved it, too. In fact, she asked me to teach her how to do it. She and her husband definitely enjoyed their practices!

Continued on page 238

Ivan the Great

Callers with desires were not exclusively Americans or Canadians, as I was reminded when I received a call from Ivan. Ivan was a twenty-three-year-old Russian who had moved to the United States a couple of years previous to his call to me. He was presently living in Columbus, Ohio, and loving it! Ivan was fascinated with American television and American women. When he described himself, in his accented English, he proudly stated that he looked like Clark Kent (**Superman**).

Ivan traveled in his sales job, and spent a lot of time in the Southern states. He enjoyed going to all-American strip clubs, and he loved lap dancing. However, he had definite opinions of certain prosecutors of whom he had become aware during his business travels. He was particularly vociferous about one in Kentucky, who evidently was giving dancers all kinds of grief about nudity versus g-strings and pasties. Ivan had definitely picked up the American tradition of openly complaining about elected officials.

Then, Ivan told me something else he had learned in America, to go down on women. He said he loved to eat pussy, and he was very proud of what he described as his "soft, gentle touch." He wanted to tell me about it, too.

In his phone fantasy, Ivan starts by eating my pussy, which he talks about in great detail. Then, he wishes for me to suck him, explaining my actions in depth. After that, we sixty-nine, until he requests that we fuck missionary style. We continue fucking until he cums.

After the sex part of the call, Ivan told me he had only seen me in magazines and brochures, but he was anxious to rent some of my movies. He belonged to an adult movies rental club, he said. He, also, wanted to join my fan club.

Ivan was definitely a nice, horny guy, who enjoyed

pleasing women as well as being pleased. I figured American women were going to enjoy this hot-blooded Russian.

* * *

Winter Heat In Saskatoon

A Canadian fan, named Andrew, called me one, cold, wintry evening. He told me he lived in Saskatoon, near the North Dakota boarder, and that he was a hospital technician.

He said the weather was so bad and the snow so high that all he wanted to do was come home from the hospital and have lots of heated sex in front of his wood-burning stove. Unfortunately, Andrew was alone, so he called me. That way he could at least fantasize about the sex in front of the stove.

Andrew told me he was both an ass and pussy man. He, also, liked tits, but they came in third, with him, he said. He really liked to enjoy the whole woman, Andrew added.

Now, Andrew is ready to heat up, for his phone fantasy sex. We are already undressed. He has

burning stove. Andrew says he wants me to touch myself all over and to play with myself in front of him. I seductively touch my breasts, and play with my pussy, describing in detail what I am doing.

Andrew gets very turned on and tells me he wants to eat my pussy. After eating my pussy for a while, he says we should "69." As I tell him the details of our "69ing," Andrew becomes hotter. Finally, in the phone fantasy, we fuck, with me laying back on the carpet, and him on top, in the traditional missionary position. At this point, Andrew orgasms.

I understood Andrew's desire for a hot body next to him during the heart of the winter in his area of Canada. He was a nice guy who took advantage of fantasy phone sex's availability, when he was feeling so sexual and was by himself. I was glad I was able to warm up his night.

* * * *

Pre-Meeting Ecstasy

All kinds of people called me from different types of environments, including a certain number who would actually call from their offices. Pat, from St. Paul, Minnesota, was one such mid-morning caller. He immediately told me he headed a building supplies company, and was so busy that he had to sneak in a little relaxation and escapism whenever and wherever it was possible. This particular morning, he was in his office, and wished for a few minutes of ecstasy before a meeting.

Pat was quickly to the point, telling me he was short on time. He said he had seen me in magazines, and had picked me because he was a tit man. Pat also told me he loved to go down on women, and that he desired I frequently call his cock "pretty" during his fantasy. Further, he requested he control the call and its pacing.

Instantly, Pat is into his fantasy by having us get undressed and sit on the gray carpeting, in front of his desk, in his office. He lies on his back, on the carpet, and tells me to sit on his face so he can eat my pussy. Pat describes eating my pussy in vivid detail. After that he indicates I am to go down on him. As I start to suck him, in his phone sex fantasy, he tells me his cock is seven inches long with a nice purple head, with swollen

veins on top of it. He wants me to lick the swollen veins, first, then, to practice my oral talents on him. "Don't forget to call it pretty," he reminds me.

Before I verbally relate very much sucking to him, he interrupts me by asking if I want to see him jerk off. Pat makes it a rhetorical question. However, I give the expected answer, not forgetting to call his cock "pretty." Then, he has me lie back, and he places his cock between my tits, and jerks off using my tits, holding and squeezing them around his cock. He continues talking about what he's doing and how it feels. When Pat finally is ready to explode, he decides to shoot all over my face. Pat cums hard and describes it as a "large load."

When Pat was completely finished, he thanked me for the brief respite from his workaholic life. He said that the next time he called, he wanted me on all fours facing him, so he could enjoy my breasts from that view. Then, he hurriedly said good-bye, until the next time.

Pat managed to get a lot into his brief call, and it was pretty apparent he was an expert at time-use efficiency. He had planned it all out, from the first hello, before he even called. I wondered if he would do the same detailed planning, from beginning to end, the next time he called. I was looking forward to finding out.

* * * *

The Graduate

My fantasy phone sex callers included men who were simply not as sexually experienced as other men in their particular age group. While the majority of men, who called, had had some sexual moments by the time they were adults, there was a certain percentage, who, for various reasons, were lacking in expertise. Sometimes, the callers would share this information with me.

Around breakfast time, one summer morning, I received a call from 23-year-old Zeke, of Columbus, Ohio. Zeke described himself as 6 feet 1 inch, 185 pounds, with blonde-brown hair and mustache, and sapphire blue eyes. He proudly added he had a 10 and a half-inch cock.

Zeke was a tits and lips man. He loved large breasts and luscious lips, and he thought I had both. Although he had not seen any of my movies, he had seen my pictures in men's magazines. He was intrigued by me, so he arranged for a call.

Zeke told me he worked in a restaurant, but had spent the last six and a half years in a Bible college, and was almost finished getting his masters degree. He was going to be a theologian and minister. At the time he had made that decision, he had decided to save himself for his wedding night. However, about a year before his call to me, that plan came to a screeching halt, when he unexpectedly "lost his cherry."

Zeke said he had been seduced by a beautiful forty-one-year-old woman, his stepmother. While he felt some guilt, he also discovered that sex was even better than his imagination. He loved it! Zeke thought of his stepmother as his sex teacher during the few encounters they shared because she literally had to demonstrate and show everything to him. However, by most standards, Zeke still felt pretty naïve and ignorant in the ways of sex. He thought of himself as still in training.

When the stepmother affair ended, Zeke realized he couldn't go back to his virginal days, as he was frequently horny since the dam had burst. He found sex on his mind almost all the time.

While sharing his background with me, Zeke was getting worked up for his fantasy, which he wanted primarily to take place in his duplex-home. Zeke gave me the details of what he wished to occur in his fantasy phone sex. Then, he was ready.

In Zeke's fantasy, I am making a personal appearance at an adult bookstore, and Zeke is there to get an autograph. We flirt with each other. I give him the impression I find him sexy, to which he responds. Then, I invite him to take me home with him. Zeke is hot and happy about doing that.

When we get to his home, I take Zeke to his bedroom (after he tells me where it is, of course).

In his bedroom, he proudly points out his very large Paul Bunyan bed.

While I am admiring his bed, I begin doing a seductive strip tease. Once I get to my stockings I have him remove them. I notice there is a large bulge in his pants, so I reach down and rub his cock through his pants. Then, I undress him and push him down on his back on his special bed.

Now, I move above Zeke's body, and rub my breasts all over his face. I offer him my nipples to suck, which he instantly does. Then, I massage his chest with my wet, hard nipples. Zeke is already in ecstasy. Next, I travel down his stomach and abdomen with my nipples still rubbing all over him. I follow with my tongue. I can now hear Zeke's hard breathing. When I arrive at his cock, I just give it some instant, light, feathery licks. I continue down to his testicles, which I suck.

At this point, Zeke interrupts me to ask that I please rim him. I raise his legs and let my tongue travel to this sensitive spot. I hear his audible breathing picking up speed. I move forward again, back to his balls and to the base of his cock. I run my tongue up the side of his cock and down the other side. Zeke begs me to suck him. So, I take his cock slowly between my lips and I move my tongue all over the head as I take it deeper into my mouth. I twist my tongue around it side to side as he goes further in my mouth. Suddenly, I go down on his cock, fast, all the way deep to my throat. While I am in the process of describing my "deep throating" to Zeke, I hear a loud groan, as he abruptly orgasms.

When Zeke could breathe normally again, he complimented me for making him feel terrific. He spoke once more about his limited sexual experiences, mainly with the stepmother. Zeke felt his shyness and his ministerial studies constantly fought his new sexual side, yet, he had decided sex had to be part of his life, now. He had tasted the forbidden fruit and the taste was too delicious, too delectable to stop eating. However, Zeke had to resolve the best way to channel it in the least destructive manner for his lifestyle and future plans. So, while he was trying to put it all together, he decided calling me was a good temporary answer. In fact, before we said our good byes, Zeke insisted on setting up a phone call with me for one week later.

Zeke was a very horny, nice guy, who wanted to help people and to save souls, but had run into an inner conflict, the kind of which he had never dreamed. I hoped he would soon find an equally horny, loving girl, so that he could marry, (celibacy was not required in his religion), and enjoy his sexuality to its fullest without the pangs of conscience. In the meantime, I knew Zeke and I would have steamy, satisfying conversations that would help fulfill his desires.

Continued from page 228

Damiano, who actually wrote **Portrait** for me, decided to use my special talent in the movie. Since movies are not filmed in sequence, my virgin sex scene was with Jamie Gillis, and it included singing and sucking.

The scene went beautifully. It was sizzling, sensuous, and humorous, too. I had changed the choice in songs though, because I was concerned I would be nervous, the first time, singing and sucking in front of the camera, and might forget the lyrics. So, I sang a song with simpler lyrics but the same effectiveness.

In the world of oral sex, I had other firsts on screen, in that same movie. There was a scene where my character, who had multiple personalities, sucked two cocks together, at the exact same time. It had never before been done successfully on camera, as it had been found too difficult. However, I knew I could do it. Damiano mostly let me direct this scene, since I was able to make it work.

"Vibrations" was another of my personal sucking inventions that I also performed in **Portrait**. I would turn my mouth into a living vibrator, which was pure ecstasy for a man. I did all kinds of vibrations, some light and delicate to strong and intense, and every type in between.

The most important thing with vibrations was to make sure the male understood it was a little noisy. Vibrations could not be done quietly, but once a man accepted that fact, he could allow himself to simply give in to the sensual delights that come from vibrations. Vibrations were truly an exciting addition to superlative sucking.

Continued on page 244

On The Road Again

At breakfast time, one morning, I received a call from Thad, a native of Portland, Maine. Thad had previously spoken to another star whose movies he had enjoyed. However, he had since seen some of my movies and was my fan, also. So, he grabbed his first, possible opportunity to talk to me, and arranged for a call.

Thad said he was a big guy, 6 feet 4 inches tall, and 235 pounds of pure muscle. He had dark curly hair and sea blue eyes. He was a pussy man, Thad added.

The reason Thad called at this particular hour was because of his career. He told me he was a trucker, and immediately after his call he was heading for New Jersey, the rest of the day, with a load of lumber. Thad always liked to have sexy fantasy calls before he left with a load. It had become a kind of tradition with him.

Thad's phone sex fantasy finds us in his queen-sized waterbed together. We are making out and he is handling me all over. Then, we undress each other, while continuously kissing and tonguing each other.

After getting naked, Thad has me sit on his face, so he can show me how talented his lips and tongue are on my pussy. Thad loves to be sucked, too. He asks me to turn around and "69" with him, with me on top. Next, I pull away and while he is lying back on the bed with a full erection, (he tells me), I spread his legs slightly and crawl between them.

This time, he gets to lose himself in my oral talents. I play with, lick and suck his balls, working my way to his cock. I run my tongue all over it, licking his hard cock, and teasing it. Now, I take his cock into my mouth, describing everything in minute detail, as I very slowly start going down on it. I give Thad all kinds of tongue action, as I take him deeper in my mouth, in his phone sex fantasy. I slowly suck my way back up

his cock. Instantly, I go back down on him hard, fast, and deep into my throat. It's apparent that Thad is extremely turned on. I continue sucking Thad, verbally, while I listen to him passionately moaning on the phone, at the same time. Finally, as I start to do "vibrations," Thad lets out a climactic cry. He sounds like he has a great orgasm!

Thad was so very nice. After the fantasy phone sex was over, he sweetly thanked me, telling me how special our conversation was to him. He told me he would be thinking about the call as he was cruising his 18-wheeler down the highway. I reminded him to keep his mind on the road. Before we hung up, Thad said to expect to hear from him again, with another load ready to go somewhere.

* * * *

Snow Bound

Cold country calls always increased during the winter months. A good-sized blizzard is what nudged Wendell to call the first time. He was snow-bound in

Cheyenne and was feeling lonesome for some sexy moments with me

Wendell was thirty-four and single. He loved women, but didn't have anyone special in his life. While he enjoyed all women his favorites were tall, leggy, and slender. He referred to himself as a leg man. However, he admired women's pussies and asses, too. He also mentioned that he took great pleasure in sexually pleasing women.

When he wasn't stuck in blizzards, Wendell was running an international military surplus business. As a result, he traveled a great deal, both in the states and overseas, and found it difficult to form any kind of lasting relationship.

On this particular night, Wendell begins his phone sex fantasy by eating my pussy. He does this in great verbal detail. He wants me to tell him how much I enjoy it. After that, he desires I suck him, and he asks that I describe all my fancy moves doing it, too. Wendell gets off while this is occurring.

Following the phone fantasy sex, Wendell talked more about his career and how hard he had worked to become successful and well-off, but he also talked about the downside to it. He missed having one woman all his own, with whom he could share love and his success. However, Wendell said I made him feel good that night, and that he would be looking forward to talking to me again.

* * * *

Troubled Welder

    I quickly discovered when doing calls, there are people who find their lives in disarray and have a need to vent, and, yet, at the same time have a desire for sexual pleasure. Eddie, in his early thirties, from Arkansas, was such a man. He called late one evening, filled with both anger and sexual desires. After saying he had seen me in **Cheri** magazine, he changed gears briefly. Eddie told me he was a high bridge welder for the Arkansas Department of Highways, and that his position required him to do a great deal of traveling around the state.

    Recently, he said, there had been some negative changes in his life. His wife of seven years had taken their two children and moved out a couple of months previous to his call. Eddie was very upset. His wife and kids were everything to him. So, he spent all his time working since they left. His wife was a virgin until they married, he said, and he had dated her for two years before proposing. Then, he bitterly mentioned they were in a custody battle for their two children.

    At this point, I figured Eddie called simply to tell his tale of woe to a non-judgmental woman, whom he felt he knew from the magazines. After all, sometimes, callers only wanted a sympathetic ear. However, about the time I thought I figured out the call, Eddie told me he had not had any sex since his wife had left him, and that he felt really horny.

At this point, the call turned to another direction.

Eddie tells me he loves oral sex. He says he especially loves to eat pussy, although he loves to be sucked too, particularly he enjoys his balls being sucked. He talks about how he is dreaming of fucking all night long with a sweet and willing woman, since he misses sex so much. Then, he asks me to suck him off. Eddie cums right away.

After his orgasm, Eddie told me it was the first time he felt good in at least two months. He said he was exhausted from releasing so much of his personal feelings to me, and from cumming, too. He asked me if he could "shoot the shit" with me occasionally.

I felt badly for Eddie. I didn't know why his marriage broke up, but it was so apparent he was in anguish. I hoped he was feeling a little better by the time we finished talking.

Continued from page 239

I used other oral-sex techniques in the movies that I had previously created in my private life, and there were some, as well, that I did not share in my movies. However, I would frequently tell callers about them if they asked.

The number of callers who would desire for me to sing a song on my finger or on a dildo was truly amazing, and their reactions were so powerful it never ceased to astonish me.

Some callers would request talking about oral sex because they had seen my stage show, which partly was an intellectual exercise on the techniques of oral sex, while remaining sexy and fun.

One of my more amusing moments, related to erotic films and oral sex, concerned the prerelease publicity for the world premiere of a wonderful cult film I made, called **S.O.S.,** which was produced by my friend, Al Goldstein, publisher of **Screw** magazine, and his partner at the time, Jim Buckley. The idea of the movie was to bring the magazine to life, on the big screen. In the movie, we did a satirization segment of the Johnny Carson Show. I was the "guest," essentially playing myself as "Jody Maxwell, the Singing Cocksucker from Missouri."

The publicist wanted to get some press about the film's world premiere in New York City, in the **New York Times**, which was too staid to do stories on openings of erotic films. So, the publicist gave the **Times** a nice head shot of me, saying I was the star, Jody Maxwell, the popular Singing Sticklicker from Missouri, a country singer, in the new comedy, **S.O.S.,** opening at a certain popular, regular (meaning non x-rated) theater. The New York Times included my picture in their paper, with all the above information under my picture, including "country singer" and the term the

"Singing Sticklicker from Missouri." Of course, I was never a country singer in my life, although the rest was accurate.

After having a few chuckles over the publicist's coup, I thought that was the end of it. Little did I know my picture was being seen all over the country by the country music radio stations, and that getting my picture in the ***Times,*** as this country singer starring in some movie, was sparking interest in places such as Nashville, Birmingham, and other cities throughout the country, including my own hometown. My phone at The Waldorf began ringing off the wall. I think just about every country station in America attempted to call me. Some were curious, many were upset they didn't have any of my records to play. A few even thought I was Loretta Lynn, because of a slight resemblance in my newspaper picture, or some other star, using a different name. Everybody wanted an interview. The calls were coming in so fast, I couldn't get away from the phone. When I tried to explain to these various stations the inaccuracy of the country singer part, they just didn't want to accept it. I finally had to put a hold on my calls because it was impossible for me to talk to all those stations. I used to wonder if Loretta Lynn got any calls asking her if she was, also, Jody Maxwell, the Singing Sticklicker from Missouri.

Continued on page 255

Lonesome in Folsom

Married, Thirty-one year old Art, from Folsom, California called one rainy, mid-morning, in the spring. Art was a virgin to fantasy phone sex, but was experienced in enjoying erotica in other forms. He had seen some of my movies, and even had a favorite, ***S.O.S.*** Art had also seen me on stage, in San Francisco, at O'Farrell Theatre. He had seen other erotic film stars there too, over the years, when he and his wife lived in San Francisco, but I was definitely number one in his mind. He had even saved the ads for my shows from the **San Francisco Chronicle.**

Art told me he had been laid off from a computer company for a little over a year, so he had lots of time on his hands. His wife, who was an executive with a telecommunications company, had been working overtime, everyday, for the previous three weeks. He had hardly seen her during that period, and she was too tired to share his desires for sex. She was still working overtime, and he was horny, he said.

Although Art declared he was feeling aroused, he was not quite ready to fulfill his phone fantasy. He wanted to chat about other topics including religion, (he was Jewish), politics, baseball, (a Giants' fan), and world affairs.

After a few comments on those topics, Art decided to describe himself. He said he was overweight, at 265 pounds. He stood 6 feet 2 inches tall and had blue eyes and curly brown-black hair. Art claimed he had a fairly large circumcised cock, and he loved to eat pussy. However, women's tits were his biggest turn on, "biggest" being the key word here. The talk about large breasts seemed to finally get Art focused on what he wanted from the call.

Art's phone fantasy begins in his king-sized waterbed. He wants me to rub my breasts all over his face and chest and down his body. After rubbing my breasts on his cock, I suck him. Then, he wants to go down on me so badly that he has me turn around, and we "69." Following this, he tells me, because he's such a big guy, he prefers me on top, sitting on his well-endowed cock. We fuck in that position, in Art's phone fantasy, while I lean forward, so that he can suck my tits, also. That sets Art off, and he erupts in orgasm.

Art was mellow after cumming, but still in a talkative mood. He told me his wife's pet nickname was Minnie Mouse and his own was Mickey. He, also, expressed a desire to take me out to dinner, not for sex, but because he genuinely liked me. Art was really very sweet and nice. I told him while I could not have dinner with him, that I truly enjoyed our conversation.

He was disappointed, but understood. However, Art did tell me he would be calling me at other times. I heard from Art occasionally for the next few years.

* * * *

Oral Only, Please

I was learning quickly there was a lot more to phone sex than callers simply having orgasms. They frequently were fans, who had seen me in movies, on stage, making personal appearances, or speaking somewhere, and loved the idea of talking to me personally and privately. Some callers just wanted to hear a friendly, female voice say nice things to them.

One of my earlier callers was Chris from Chicago. Chris was a true fan of mine, having seen several of my movies and having attended one of my personal appearances. He was a very courteous, polite twenty-nine-year-old, whose main interest was oral sex. Chris requested that I suck him, and do some specialty techniques he had previously seen me do in some of my movies.

In his fantasy, Chris meets me and I think he is

terrific. So, we go to his place and I immediately want to suck him. That thrills him. We go to his bedroom where I proceed to describe in very great detail the oral sex that I perform on him. I also do the oral specialty techniques he requested. Chris has an orgasm during the verbalizing of my specialty techniques. It's evident he loves it!

Chris was a very happy man by the end of the call. Just before we finished speaking, Chris informed me he also loved anal sex, but that we could save that for the next time.

Like a majority of the men who called me, Chris gave me a detailed description of his penis. He did not try to come across like the late John Holmes, but gave what I would call a modest description of his penis. I discovered pretty quickly that most men, who called, seemed to enjoy describing their penises to me.

* * * *

The Shy Exhibitionist

Tony, from Palm Beach, Florida, called one evening, with the desire to be seduced, and to do things he ordinarily would not do, including in front of other people. He mentioned it was important he that he get to eat my pussy in the fantasy, as well. Tony talked about his extreme shyness and his travels. He mentioned that he frequently visited New York. His family lived in New York, he said, and he would like to see my stage show, sometime, when I was appearing there. Tony told me he loved oral sex both as the giver and as the receiver, but primarily as the giver. However, because of his shyness he didn't get out with women all that much to enjoy that pleasure.

His fantasy starts in The Mitchell Brothers' O'Farrell Theatre, in San Francisco, where I am starring in The Kopenhagen Lounge.

Tony comes in and sits on one of the couches in the room.

I enter the showroom and dance and visit with the audience. I am dressed in an aqua, silky, slinky gown trimmed in lace. After doing a very seductive dance, I go up to Tony in the audience, and I rub my breasts in his face. Then, I pull him up from his seat and take him to the middle of the room. I sit him on the end of a velvet ottoman. I lie back on an additional ottoman and spread my legs and offer him my pussy. I reach up and pull his head down and tell him to eat me. He is so turned on he enthusiastically eats me, much to the envy of rest of the audience.

Next, Tony wants to go to a "swing," so I place us at a well-known swingers' club's monthly function, where there are about 400 naked people enjoying themselves.

I get Tony to undress me. Then, I undress him. We are in a suite crowded with people who are watching us.

I lie on a bed and pull him down to me. I stroke his cock and tell him to eat me, which he does. As I start cumming, I have him go inside me.

When Tony is about to have an orgasm, in the fantasy, I have him pull out and release his juices on my stomach. Tony is so turned on by the entire fantasy that he has an actual, huge orgasm, on the phone, at that point.

After the phone sex fantasy, Tony told me how great he felt, almost liberated from his shyness. Tony was not the only person from whom I received calls because of shyness. Lots of shy people would call for phone sex. It was always fun to hear them enjoy themselves.

* * * *

Heated Waterbed

Woody, from Grosse Pointe Shores, Michigan, called early one morning after awakening from sexy, hot dreams. It was cold there, he said, and he wanted to warm up to the heat he had been feeling in his dream-sleep. Woody described himself as twenty–one years old, 6 feet 2 inches, with dark brown hair, matching dark brown eyes, and a nice body. He added he had an excellent job at Ford Motor Plant.

Woody was calling from his waterbed in his lovely lakeshore home, he told me, and he had a fire going in his bedroom fireplace because it was so cold outside.

His two favorite loves, after cars and the lake, were older women and big tits, Woody said. I asked him what qualified as an older woman, for him. He told me any woman over twenty-five matched that qualification. Woody continued to say what turned him on the most was sexually pleasing women. In fact, he proudly described his long tongue, and his ability to give great "face," as he put it. Listening to him, it was clear he was ready for his sexy phone fantasy.

Woody and I are in his waterbed, kissing, and he is also fingering my pussy, at the same time. I am stroking his cock while all this is happening. He begins working his way down me, squeezing and sucking my breasts. Woody pushes them

together and sucks both nipples at once. I keep on stroking his throbbing hard cock. He continues down me, with an active tongue, all the way.

When Woody reaches my pussy, he is so excited he groans with pleasure. He uses his talented tongue on my pussy until he can hardly stand it. Then, he turns around and I suck his hard cock, while he continues going wild on my pussy with his tongue and lips.

Finally, Woody wants to fuck, briefly, with him lying back and me on top. Following that, he requests to do his favorite position, doggie style. While we are doing it doggie style, in his phone sex fantasy, he cums hard!

Woody was anxious to say goodbye shortly after his orgasm. So, our follow up conversation was very short. However, he did stick around long enough to tell me how much he enjoyed the experience. He also said he was going back to sleep as soon as we hung up. I felt certain Woody would have a peacefully sound sleep for rest of the early morning hours.

One year, while I was with ***Cheri***, my editor, the late Peter Wolff, approached me with an extraordinary idea for something to include in the magazine as a Christmas gift for the readers. He wanted me to consider making a singing and sucking Christmas record at a prestigious recording studio in New York City. Of course, I would choose the person with whom I would be doing this, if I agreed to do it.

After giving it some thought, I said yes. I asked my friend and fellow actor, Don Allen, with whom I had worked in ***S.O.S.***, to be my "supplying-the-instrument" partner in this recording. I knew Don could nicely handle the pressure.

When we all arrived at this famous recording studio, we were greeted by the sound production people in an extremely professional manner. Peter had previously talked to their people explaining what he had in mind, and telling them that I would only be accompanied by a middle-aged male pianist. I would be singing on Don's instrument. Amazingly, this well-known recording studio had agreed to this unusual recording.

As we were getting set up in the studio, one of the sound people, a young, good-looking guy, came out to place the mikes for me. Since I was standing, he came over and put the mikes at a normal recording height, around four and a half feet, and inquired if that was acceptable.

Since I was somewhat nervous to be in this house of music where so many famous singers had recorded their hits, I suddenly realized I wasn't sure what position in which I wanted to be, when I did my singing. First of all, I wanted to be comfortable, I thought. So, looking the young guy straight in the eyes I solemnly asked him if he could please lower the mikes to about eighteen inches high. His disbelieving facial expression was funny, but I didn't laugh. I was too busy checking the new height of the microphones.

I had decided that Don would be more comfortable lounging on the carpeted floor, and I could get better angles, clarity, and tone with the mikes while doing my special brand of singing.

The sound production people went to their glass booth, leaving both the pianist and Don with me. After the pianist and I discussed a few things, I joined Don on the floor. Then, when everyone else was ready to go, I performed my musical magic, by singing a couple of popular holiday songs. Don responded as I had expected. The pianist did an excellent job. Everybody seemed happy.

Only one time, while I was singing did I look over at the production booth, and I did notice absolute amazement on the faces of the sound guys. However, I put it out of my mind for the time being.

When we were finished and they had checked the recordings, the same young guy, who had previously assisted me, came into the recording room, again. This time, stammering, he asked me for my autograph. While I was signing it for him, he did the strangest thing. He unzipped his pants and pulled out his own very hard erection, and asked me if I would consider singing another song.

Startled, I nicely told him to put his penis back in his pants, that he had to be professional. I was there to make a record, and that was all.

Red-faced, he profusely apologized and told me that my singing was the most wonderful thing he had ever seen or heard in his life, and that he was totally mesmerized by me. Don, and Peter Wolff, who had joined us, were trying not to laugh, but also felt great empathy for the young guy. Actually, I felt somewhat badly for him, too, but knew this was one fantasy he was not getting fulfilled. Later, I wondered how he ever lived down his behavior with his fellow workers, who saw the whole incident from the glass booth. I also thought it was just the logically weird conclusion to this very surreal, recording day.

Over the years people have asked me if I had any personal philosophy when it came to cocksucking or fellatio. My answer has been unequivocally yes!

My attitude since I first became aware of the act was to attain all the knowledge I could about cocksucking. I believed, and still believe, that with knowledge comes understanding and, thusly, appreciation of this act that so many men absolutely love. My initial desire was to be able to please some special man in my life by being the best I could be. I realized I had to really know all about it to attain my own goal.

Of course, I could simply do what instinct told me to do. However, I found that quickly unacceptable. I discovered that too many women sucked their spouses or lovers, but they were actually afraid of the penis. The women did what they must, and hoped it would be over as quickly as possible, as either a prelude to intercourse, some other sex act, or an oral climax.

Women, all too often, didn't even look at what they were putting in their mouths when it came to sucking. They were either afraid to see, or didn't want to see, these exciting penises, even if they were deeply in love with the men to whom they belonged. So, they kept their eyes closed the whole time. They used their hands a lot to speed them up and get the "chore" completed as rapidly as possible. Many women thought it was a necessary duty in their lives.

Then, there were the women who did like it, but thought it took away something from the lovemaking by really knowing all about the penis and cocksucking. They thought just doing it was good enough.

Again, they were wrong.

There is so much feeling, love, and passion between two people in love, when they know all the ways to bring ultimate pleasure to each other. Plus, knowledgeable lovers, who are enjoying the supreme delights, know when there is genuine enthusiasm, and pleasure, from their partners who are performing these acts upon them. This in itself adds to the recipient partner's satisfaction.

For people not in love, but having passionate sex, knowing what they are doing is still superior to ignorance in their bedroom performances.

So, ultimately, intellectual curiosity, sensual interest and enthusiasm, and, of course, my goal, (the desire to share intense pleasure with a lover or spouse), had been the primary forces in my learning all I was able about oral sex before I ever got into erotica. There was a certain mystique associated with it, and I was completely determined to break through that aura and learn everything I could.

I read books by medical professionals, psychologists, sex therapists, and anyone who seemed intellectually knowledgeable on the subject.

Finally, with my own personal passions and desires to be a better lover, in my private life, I used the knowledge I had gained to achieve my personal goal.

Phone sex, (as did my columns and shows), sometimes gave me the opportunity to help lovers achieve a new high in their oral lovemaking because of my knowledge and experiences.

Likewise, I always felt the callers who wanted the cocksucking, erotic fantasies happily finished their calls in blissful states.

When it came to oral sex and callers, there were quite a few who called because their fantasies involved satisfying women. Just as I would receive calls for how-to lessons in sucking, I would receive even more how-to calls for eating pussy. Some men who called had no experience in this area, and they desired to learn how to do it. The fact is it is very difficult to teach men over the phone how to successfully eat pussy, if they have never been face-to-pussy, previously. However, I think I was pretty successful at it, all things considered.

The first thing with the non-experienced at pussy eating was the same as with the non-experienced at cocksucking. Get them over their fears of the vaginal area. Pussies don't really have teeth, except if they are four-legged cats.

When the men understood this was only as

mysterious an area for them as their cocks were for the women, those callers seemed to feel better. Some actually wrote notes on how to do it properly. Others got incredibly excited by the possibilities. Teaching callers to realize the pleasure and enjoyment they could bring women by this means, and to themselves, also, as a result, was always satisfying to me.

A number of callers wanted to talk about how they would like to do this to me. Frequently, during those calls, the callers would want to do most of the talking. Those particular calls were interesting because I learned so much more how lots of men actually saw pussy eating from their viewpoints. Since they were people unknown to me personally, and they typically wanted to impress me, they were usually pretty honest, I thought, with their own opinions on the proper ways to eat pussy.

Frequently, such men would tell me about experiences, bad and good, in this area with wives, former wives, girlfriends, or other women whose pussies had been treated to this potential delight.

There were callers, also, who wanted badly to do this to the women they loved or with whom they were involved, but their women wouldn't let them. The ladies had hang-ups about it. So, they would call and ask for fantasy scenarios where they would be successful with their special women.

Many men loved eating pussy so much that they were totally fulfilled by talking to me about it, while others included it, or wanted it incorporated by me, as one of the multiple facets in their fantasies.

Continu

A Perfect Cut

I received a call, one afternoon, from Burt, who was living in Springfield, Illinois, at the time. Immediately, Burt told me he was a native Texan, but, because of his career as a diamond distributor, had lived in several different parts of the country, including New York and California.

Burt portrayed himself as a shy guy, who adored beautiful, sexy women, who were a little assertive. After seeing one of my movies in New York, he decided he must talk to me because he felt I could be the type of woman he liked.

Eventually, Burt began telling me the things that turned him on. He said that he liked lacy, frilly bras and panties on a woman. He told me he loved breasts, and oral sex. He was crazy about "69ing," too.

After discussing his favorite turn ons, he was ready for phone fantasy sex.

I have on a sheer, sexy, lace-trimmed aqua teddy, which Burt admires, while we are lying on the bed.
Burt pulls down the thin straps of my teddy

and briefly plays with my breasts. Then, he unsnaps the crotch of my teddy. He pushes the open pieces of material away from my pussy, and reaches behind me with his hands, and squeezes my ass. While doing that, he eats my pussy.

Following the oral sex, Burt tells me he wants me to masturbate, while he stands there and watches me. This idea excites him so much, he decides to jerk off standing over me, as he continues watching my actions. He does this until he climaxes.

Burt was an enjoyable caller, a truly nice guy, with whom it was fun to talk. He clearly liked sex and various sexual activities, but it was, also, obvious that he liked to watch. He got turned on as much from watching as he did from participating – at least, on this particular occasion. Burt told me he would be checking out more of my movies in the future.

* * * *

Office Seduction

Dan, a Real Estate Developer, from Miami, gave me a call from his office, one evening. Everybody was gone for the day, and he had been finishing up some paper work. When that was out of the way, his mind wandered to more pleasant thoughts, like making love.

He described himself as slender at 6 feet and 165 pounds, with dark brown hair and brown-black eyes. Dan said he was an "everything" man when it came to women, but he was especially turned on by a woman's smile. After the smile, he thought his most favorite parts of a woman were her breasts, nipples, and ass, in that order. Dan added that he was crazy about oral sex, too, as both the giver and the receiver.

Making beautiful women happy was one of his ongoing goals, Dan told me. He had seen me in person, and I fit in that category, he said. On this occasion, he wanted to make love with me, and he desired to make me feel very good.

Dan's phone sex fantasy takes place where he really is, in his office. He kisses me and fondles my breasts through my red silk blouse. Dan leads me over to his brown leather couch, where he continues kissing me. He unbuttons my blouse, and takes it off me. I unzip his pants and pull his cock out. I start sucking him while he unfastens and removes my red satin bra. As I continue sucking him, he pushes up my skirt and pulls off my matching red panties and fingers me.

He is extremely hot, now, and he wants me equally hot. So, Dan pulls away from me, and lays me back on his couch. Then, he spreads my legs wide and eats me. He brings me to an orgasm, and he immediately wishes to climax on my breasts and face, in his fantasy. He cums hard.

Dan was a fun guy with whom to have a call. He seemed caring and personable, and even had a sexy voice. His erotic fantasy was hot and so was he. I liked talking with him and hoped to hear from him again.

* * * *

Executive Runner

One Monday evening, I received a call from Stan, of Atlanta, Georgia. Stan described himself as a divorced, 5-foot-10-inch runner, with a 7-inch cock. He told me he was an executive with Georgia Pacific, which kept his life at a high intensity level. Stan, also, told me he loved women, but didn't have a lot of time for them, unfortunately.

The perfect woman, according to Stan, had long legs, first, and long hair, second. His preference was for women on the thin side, as well, but those long legs were definitely the most important parts to him. In addition, he characterized himself as a lingerie freak.

Stan's phone fantasy begins with me sitting in the back seat of a car, wearing a cute short dress. I'm leaning back in the seat with my legs spread wide apart and my sexy, sheer, blue, silk panties are showing. He comes over to the car to speak to me and he sees my long legs in my high heels and he can't keep his eyes off my panties' smooth crotch. He asks me if we could get together the following night. I tell him yes.

The next night, Stan has me wearing an exquisite, long, black dress with a halter-top. It is split high up the middle of the front. So, with every move I make, a lot of leg shows.

After an evening of nightclubbing and dancing we end up at his place. While sitting on his couch, drinking wine, Stan plays with my exposed legs, running his hands over and up them. Then, he touches my breasts through the halter-top and makes my nipples hard. At this point, Stan slowly undresses me, except for my sheer, black, silk panties. Next, he sucks my breasts. Following that, he lays me back on the couch and he gently spreads my legs wide. Now, he gets between my legs and he eats my pussy through my panties. He continues doing this for a while. Finally, Stan tells me he wants me to get off, which, in the fantasy, I do. That sets him off with an explosive orgasm.

Following Stan's fantasy, he told me he, also, liked to make love with a woman with her panties on, but with the crotch pulled to the side. He said doggie style was his favorite position, too, because he could stroke the woman's legs while having sex with her. However, Stan's ultimate fantasy and desire was the one we had just finished.

Stan came on in a very sexy fashion, and he obviously loved to please women, which made him certainly okay in my mind! I knew I would enjoy hearing from him again.

* * * *

New York Quickie

Steve called just after midnight, one late winter evening. He was very anxious to reach me, and told me he was so pleased he lucked out. I had talked to Steve on many occasions, so the introductions were unnecessary.

I already knew that Steve lived in New York City, and was in the clothing business. He was married, but there were problems. He had told me before that he was about 6 feet tall, weighed 180 pounds, had brown hair and hazel eyes.

This particular night, when Steve called, he had

just arrived home after battling a nasty snowstorm. That didn't deter his sexual appetite, however. Steve's ultimate fantasy was to make love to an erotic film star, and for her to think he was the best lover of all. This night, though, that was not a high priority with him. He was just plain super horny, as he put it. He wanted to go down on me and to "69," he said. He wanted a touch of foreplay but not a whole lot, this time. Steve was in such a hurry he was talking very fast, much more so than usual. So, I figured we should get right to his fantasy.

We start out with some quick cuddles and kisses. Then, he sucks my breasts for a matter of seconds. Steve quickly moves down to my pussy, and begins eating me. He asks me to do all the talking. I continue describing what he is doing. While I am doing this, I hear him moaning. Then, he cums hard, very quickly.

I was fascinated because I had had many calls with Steve and had never heard him like this before. He was extremely hot from the moment we began talking, no doubt before we even began conversing. Then, after he came, Steve told me he was expecting a woman over in a few minutes. I had to laugh because I couldn't figure out what he was thinking or doing. Anyway, our whole conversation, on this night, lasted a maximum of three minutes. I decided I would ask Steve about his atypical call the next time we talked.

* * * *

The Ultimate Dream Wake Up

Jake, from Little Rock, Arkansas, called me one balmy afternoon, feeling happy and frisky. He told me it was his 42nd birthday, and he decided to give himself a birthday present, a call with me! Jake told me he had seen my movies, read my magazine columns and stories, and had previously enjoyed watching me on stage in Kansas City, Missouri. Over the years, he had become a truly avid fan, he noted.

The first thing I noticed about Jake was that he had a really hot, sultry, bedroom voice, the kind that could give goose bumps to any woman. I remember thinking this fellow could do voice-over commercials and sell almost anything to anybody, but especially to women. However, unfortunately, that wasn't his field. Jake told me he worked for the local phone company, in Little Rock, and he had taken the day off to celebrate his birthday.

I listened to Jake's incredibly sexy voice as he described himself to me. He said he had dark brown, wavy hair, and sky blue eyes, and that he stood about 5 feet 9 inches tall and weighed around 175 pounds. Jake added he was rock hard muscle -- everywhere.

He continued, saying that he was half-Italian and half-German, which he thought made him a strong, hot lover. In fact, he talked laughingly about his pussy-eating prowess being the result of his Italian half. Jake said he loved hard fucking, too, and that came from the German half.

Jake's marriage hadn't worked out, and he had had lots of women. In spite of all that, he was a highly sexual, idealistic romantic, and wanted to be with his own soul mate, he explained. That had not happened yet, so Jake was on the phone.

Jake was ready to talk about his phone fantasy. He had had a dream that was such a turn on, he wanted to share it with me. He was going to do the major part of verbalizing it because he was more intimate with his own dream.

We are in bed together, asleep. I am angry with him for some unknown reason. As a result, I am lying on my side facing away from him.

He awakens and is watching me sleep.

I have on a sheer little blue silk gown. It's moved up to the middle of my ass, while I am sleeping. My legs are slightly bent.

Jake wants to make up. He carefully moves over to me and moves down the bed, so his head is level with my pussy, yet he remains behind me. Jake raises my gown to my waist. He starts licking my pussy from behind.

I awaken feeling his talented tongue dancing on my pussy as he darts it in and out and moves it all over that area. Jake pushes my legs further up as he continues.

I try to turn over, but I can't. He has me locked in this side position away from him, and he continues to lick all my pussy, and then he concentrates on the hottest spot.

Jake goes into great detail about what he would do, and how he would do it. He reaches up and gently pulls on my nipples too, occasionally. (The gown is up above my breasts at this point). I get very hot in the fantasy and try to turn over, but he still won't let me. He won't let me do anything, but just respond and enjoy. Finally, in the phone fantasy, I can't take it anymore, so I explode with a terrific orgasm.

Jake isn't done yet. Now, he tells me he wants to lick and eat my juices, my cum. He loves it, he says. Then, he quickly turns me over on my back, and he raises my legs very high. Now, Jake fucks me with his brickbat, hard cock, doing strong, deep thrusts. He explodes inside me!

Following Jake's super orgasm, he was very mellow. He chatted a little longer about his appreciation of women, and his desire to be with his special woman. Jake talked about his admiration for my various talents, too. He reiterated how much pleasure I had brought him over the years. As we were ending the call, Jake told me I would find him to be frequently on my phone in the future.

Continued from page 260

Discussing the best styles and methods of pussy eating, or cunnilingus, with such a large and diverse number of people, one-on-one, could be a challenge. The number of men who did not know the proper words for different parts of the woman's vaginal area was surprising to me. Then, there were callers who were clueless where certain special parts of the pussy were located, that especially set women off, and could cause orgasms.

Trying to communicate those particulars over the phone was sometimes really humorous. However, I tried to keep the smile away from my voice. After all, this was serious business. I was giving more women a chance to be unknowingly grateful to me, if I could get their men on the right pussy path.

As a woman, who appreciated receiving this delight, I also took advantage of the opportunity to pass along some no-nos.

One of the most important, in my opinion, was don't rub a rough after-five shadow all over that tender area of a woman. A beard burn is a very painful reminder of a possibly wonderful moment. If a man's face were not smooth and soft, then, I would tell him to use his lips and tongue to full advantage, but no face rubbing in that area. Any woman who has ever suffered the beard burn would no doubt say the moment's ecstasy wasn't worth the several days of suffering, afterward.

To "sixty-nine" was another extremely popular desire envisioned by callers. The possibility of both partners satisfying and being satisfied at the exact same moment appealed to many callers as a semi-exotic, perfect sex act. Many callers who were interested in this had either unsuccessfully attempted to do it; or had done it, and loved it!

Others weren't quite sure how to sixty-nine, but thought it would be the ultimate oral-sex experience.

Continued on page 281

Sean's Favorite Couch

I received a call, one night, from Sean, who had recently moved from Michigan to Bridgeport, Connecticut. He said his company had just transferred him and he was lonely. Sean told me he was very much into sex and was easily turned on. Those were his reasons he gave for calling that night.

He described himself as having an Irish-American

dad and an Armenian mother. Sean claimed he had his mother's looks, with curly dark-brown hair and deep blue eyes. He said he was he was average height and weight.

He talked about his attraction to me. He had seen some of my pictures and layouts, and he mentioned how much he liked my "long legs, really nice hair, and pretty pussy." Sean added that he thought I was beautiful. I thought to myself that this was a very nice, sweet-talking guy!

Then, Sean began telling me his phone sex fantasy. He wanted to make love to me in his home. I could tell he had all the details worked out ahead of the call.

After having spent the evening out, we end up at Sean's place. Upon entering his home, we come into a front hall. In the hall, Sean doesn't waste any time. He makes out with me, kissing and tonguing me. He fondles my breasts through my black cocktail dress. We move into his living room and sit on the couch where he continues to kiss me. While doing that, he unfastens his pants and pulls out his cock. Then, he takes my hand and puts it on his hot, hard cock. He pushes lightly down on my head, indicating he wants me to suck him. I bend over, and stretch my body out, and suck him. He wants me to include a great amount of detail in describing my sucking.

After I suck him for a while, he reaches for me to turn around, which I do. While I continue to suck him, he pulls off my panties, leaving my garter belt and stockings alone. Sean asks me to leave on my hi heels. He decides to take my dress off me, at this point. He also completely loses his pants. Then, he encourages me to suck him some more as he begins eating me.

We continue "69ing," until he wants to fuck me. Sean turns around and immediately enters me, with my legs high and spread apart. After a while, he pulls out, has me turn around again, and put my legs on the floor. He kneels on the floor in front of me, spreads my legs apart and eats me, again. Now, he fucks me in that same position, where he is half on the floor and half on me. Sean is close to cumming, but he wants to do one more thing, in his fantasy. So, he pulls out, again, briefly.

He grabs a pillow off the couch, puts it on the floor, and gets me to lay on the carpeting, with my buttocks on the pillow. Sean fucks me for the third time. This time, he raises my legs so high that I wrap them around his upper back. This way he can deeply penetrate me. He has a tremendous orgasm while we are in this position.

Sean was definitely a detail man when it came to sex. It was also pretty obvious that he took pleasure in making his partner feel good. I figured he probably approached non-fantasy sex the same way since he seemed a pleasant, considerate guy. Sometimes, it was hard to understand a good guy like Sean being lonely. I hoped he felt a lot less lonely when the call ended.

* * * *

Rocket Man

At some point, everyone needs a break from the pressures of work and daily life, even if it is only through a brief moment of fantasy or play. My caller, Adam, was ready for a pleasant pause from his normal schedules, when he called me late one night.

Although Adam, a long-time fan, was originally from Seattle, Washington, his career had placed him in California. Adam said he considered himself a workaholic, who loved his work, but he found it extremely stressful, too. He was a propulsion engineer, who designed rocket motors. Adam worked for a private company, but his work actually was ultimately for the government and NASA. He couldn't even discuss most of it because it was secret.

Adam described himself as 5 feet 9 inches tall, and as having medium brown hair and hazel eyes. He was in his early thirties and single, he said.

Since Adam had previously told the screener he wanted some mild domination, (which she had repeated to me), I had been thinking in those terms. However, while talking with me, he said he had changed his mind. Instead, he wanted to make love with me. Then, he told me he loved women's pussies and asses. He definitely was not a breast man, he added. Adam was apparently ready for his sexy fantasy.

We begin his fantasy phone sex at his apartment, where we listen to some soft rock, while drinking white wine. Then, we move into his candle-lit bedroom. Adam kisses me with long, deep kisses, while unfastening our clothing. After we are undressed, we continue making out on his king-sized bed. Then, I begin licking his chest, his stomach, working my way down his body. When I arrive at his genitals, I start gently licking and sucking his balls. I move up to his cock and I suck it, giving a detailed description of my actions.

Now, Adam desires to reciprocate. So, I turn over, lying on my back. He spreads my legs wide and licks my hot pussy. After a little of this, Adam wishes to "69," which we immediately do.

Following all that, Adam requests I sit on his throbbing cock, and ride him hard. Finally, he has me get on my hands and knees, and we fuck doggie style. Almost immediately he explodes in my pussy.

After his orgasm, Adam thanked me very nicely for relaxing him and giving him some escapism for a little while. He was feeling exceptionally laid back, he said.

I found Adam to be an exceedingly nice guy.

I enjoyed talking with him. He worked hard and played little. Adam missed his friends and family in Washington, and didn't even have time to find and build a relationship with a girl, in the less populated areas of California in which he was living and working. I liked Adam and I hoped I would get to talk to him again.

* * * *

Lookin' for Love

Sometimes, busy men call between romances in their private lives. They want to connect with a female, and, yet, they haven't the time to go through finding, meeting, and courting women. In some cases, they have seen the woman they are calling, in films and magazines. Chris was such a man, a thirty-year-old bachelor, from Boston, who had been a fan of mine for years. He owned an upscale restaurant and lounge and put in long weeks. For a sideline, he taught martial arts, and even competed professionally. Chris described himself as 5 feet 7 inches, and 165 pounds, with black hair and brown eyes, and a straight, wide, circumcised penis. He was also a collector of both erotic films and men's magazines.

Chris was something of a romantic, as well. He mentioned he was very well off, and would like to fly me to Boston to be entertained by him, suggesting dinner and a show for starters. Chris also told me he wanted to make love to me, that satisfying a woman was as important to him as being satisfied. Initially, Chris wanted lots of small talk so we could get to know each other.

To prepare for the call with me, Chris had one of my men's magazine layouts spread out in front of him. He had one of my movies in his VCR, as well, but turned off the sound, so he could look at me and watch me as we talked. Chris had made arrangements for a long call, too. Finally, we came to the heart of the call.

Chris tells me he loves stockings and spiked hi heels on a woman, and requests that I wear these continuously in the fantasy. He takes me to bed, after a night on the town. There, he seduces me, and licks my entire body, especially the pussy. Then, he wants to "69."

As we continue, he fingers me and rims me, in the fantasy. Finally, he asks me to suck him off. That completely satisfies him.

Following his orgasm, Chris resumed trying to persuade me to come and visit him. He continued to chat with me as if we were lovers. It was obvious that in his fantasy he didn't simply want sex; he also wanted a relationship. Chris persisted in his desires to develop a special relationship with me, (to no avail), throughout his calls, which continued for a few years.

* * * *

Speedboat #69

I always enjoyed talking to friendly, personable Mel, from Tampa, Florida. He was a divorced thirty-nine-year-old, who described himself as having dark brown hair and blue eyes. He said he was 6 feet tall, weighed 182 pounds, and was very physical. Also, Mel claimed he was "fairly well-endowed" with a large 9-inch cock.

Mel also shared with me his unusual occupation. He said that he was an offshore boat racer, racing 50-foot ocean speedboats. He spent a good deal of time talking about the kind of lifestyle he lived with that kind of career. Mel even told me that he was a judge at a wet tee-shirt contest, sponsored by the racing tour.

With all that was happening in Mel's life, he did not have a regular lady. He had seen my movie, **Expose Me Lovely**, liked it and began calling me. He was a regular of mine for many years.

Mel tells me, up front, his favorite sexual things. He's a tit man, and he loves oral sex. He likes a finger in his anus while being sucked, and he prides himself on his versatility in bed. Mel loves to try new things, he says. He loves to "69." Mel enjoys it so much he prefers it to intercourse.

While telling me his sexual preferences, Mel gets turned on. He decides he wants to eat me. He continues telling me how he is doing it, in great detail. Then, he desires to "69," his very favorite sexual activity. He asks me to suck him as hard as possible, and he requests that I finger his butt while we're doing it. Soon, he climaxes while we are still "69ing."

After Mel's orgasm, we chatted some more about some of his other sexual experiences. He had met women over the years, who were into different kinds of sexual activities. Some, he tried with them; others, he did not try.

Mel came across as a charming, worldly guy, whose lifestyle, sometimes, left him wanting a woman, without any on the horizon, the way he saw it. Then, he would call me for sexual phone fantasies. We always had fun talking over the years.

Obviously, the problems with the sixty-nine position did not exist in fantasy phone calls. On the other hand, those callers who wanted to solve their real-world problems doing this position, found they were usually resolved after we talked about it.

Most problems with the sixty-nine position are logistical; getting literally into place, and being comfortable, besides, is not always easy.

In addition, two people who really care enough about each other to give their very best, are torn between concentrating on opposite parts of their bodies. Yes, it can be wonderfully enjoyable, but the people who are doing it have to be able to give what they can, and accept what they are able, together, simultaneously. It's fantastic, but it can be tough to do.

Oral sex in any of its various forms was involved in a great many callers' fantasies. Whether it was exclusively oral sex or just one of the many parts of the sexual acts of the callers, it always thrilled them. The calls generally pleased me, as well, because I knew they were happy when they hung up, and, hopefully, more knowledgeable on one of the truly great sexual pleasures.

CHAPTER 7

THE CABOOSE

Sometimes callers would have erotic fantasies involving a kind of sex with which they were less experienced or not even experienced at all. In some cases, they were plenty knowledgeable, but they had only rare opportunities to enjoy their favorite sexual act.

For others, it was the very nature of the "forbidden fruit" syndrome that attracted some callers to this fantasy.

Historically, this particular sexual act, anal intercourse, used to be considered taboo, and that actually made the act more fascinating and desirable to a number of people. In some quarters, the taboo viewpoint still stands today.

Until June, 2003, a number of states still had laws relating to anal intercourse. However, that June, the United States Supreme Court ruled those laws unconstitutional when it pertained to two people doing this sexual act behind closed doors.

Previously, if these laws had been strictly enforced, there would not have been enough prisons to hold all those who had experimented with anal sex. As for the states that only monetarily fined the people instead, (the people who would have eventually been found guilty of sodomy), those states would have been rich with a never-ending source of revenue. As it was, most states chose to ignore a generally unenforceable law, except in rare, specific cases.

Initially, the primary reason there were such laws was to discourage homosexuality. Some states actually stated in their laws that anal sex was prohibited by two people of the same gender, referring to males, obviously. Other states' laws specified "anybody" who engaged in anal sex, but in reality these were considered anti-homosexuality laws, regardless of the wording.

Anal sex origins go back to ancient Greek and Roman times, according to the writings of the early philosophers and playwrights. Artwork depicting anal intercourse in ancient times has been found by archeologists in ruins from those earlier ages.

Yet, with all the knowledge, history, and controversy surrounding it, anal sex is still written and spoken with shock value treatment in the entertainment arena --

the remnants of the old taboos still hanging around. There is only one exception -- hardcore, erotic movies.

In the world of erotic movies, there are generally two kinds of films involving anal sex. The less common type, which rarely have mainstream erotic actors and actresses in them, are made strictly for the prurient satisfaction of people who are extreme, anal sex lovers or fetishists. These movies are usually one-dimensional and lacking in story line.

The second, and more popular kind, often consider this kind of sex scene as a natural and somewhat necessary part of the movie. Adult movies, catering to couples, almost always have a heterosexual, anal sex scene.

Continued on page 291

The Gentle Doctor

During the years I was creating phone sex fantasies, I would hear from all kinds of callers, and regardless of some similarities among many of them, each in his (or her) own way was unique. I never permitted myself to forget that.

One caller, named Mickey, brought that home to me. Mickey, a St. Louis fellow, told me he was a veterinarian, who specialized in emergencies, zoos, and small animals, but didn't treat birds. He, also, casually, stated he was in a wheelchair, having been shot up in Vietnam.

Then, he moved on to discussing cat and dog pregnancies with me. We talked about my dogs, and his dog. He said he wished he could have a nice proper portrait shot of me with his Irish Setter to hang in his office.

Mickey chatted with me as if we were long lost friends. He said he had been very much in love with a girl when he went to Vietnam, but lost her because of his permanent injuries. He mentioned that people "don't want to get involved with people, physically, in a chair." As a result, he had a call girl in his life.

At this point, Mickey abruptly changed directions in our conversation. He spoke of my movies and how much he loved them. He said he was into asses, and oral sex, but primarily asses. He claimed he was in love with my ass after watching it in several movies. He told me I had "an hourglass ass, which blew his mind." He even thought my "ass gleamed."

After those comments, Mickey says he wishes to have me doggie style, which is one of his two favorite sexual positions. While we are doing this, Mickey talks about how much he enjoys it.

Next, he decides to change sexual activities and to do his other favorite one with me, which is anal sex. Mickey takes that slowly because he says that anal sex should be gentle. He continues taking me anally, in his phone sex fantasy, until he is fulfilled.

I was certain Mickey enjoyed himself, equally as much for chatting with me as for the phone sex. He was truly a nice guy, who had gone through a lot, yet, was a survivor. I was glad Mickey was a fan of mine. I looked forward to hearing from him again.

* * * *

Let Me Talk Sexy

In the very early hours, one morning, I received a call from David, a long time, "adoring" fan since he had first seen me in movies. David, of Newark, New Jersey, was previously a professional actor, but, now, was a computer salesman. Although computers were his business, he refused to own one personally, he emphasized to me. However, own one or not, he also was a computer consultant.

David was getting over a divorce, but felt it was worth it, because he was so unhappy, even though he had still cared for his ex-wife at the time of the divorce. He just wanted to get on with his life. David was optimistic that the right woman for him was out there somewhere.

Even though David was only thirty-two, he described his brown and gray hair as quickly thinning. He further portrayed himself as having big brown eyes, standing 6 feet tall, and weighing 180 pounds. David added he was a leg and "tush" man, but any woman that attracted him also had to have presence and class.

Then, he was ready for his phone sex fantasy.

David and I are in bed together. I am lying back, fingering my pussy, while he watches me. He leans over and kisses me and plays with my breasts. Next, David lies on his side and I begin licking his balls, and sucking his cock. I do this only briefly, because suddenly he interrupts me and takes over the talking. David tells me he wants me hot. He pushes me back on the bed and begins heavy pussy eating. Then, he rims me in detail. David continues the talking. Finally, David fucks me missionary style. From there, he raises my ass and he takes me anally. He is breathing hard and whispering, now. David says he wants me to cum, just before he moans in orgasm.

After the phone sex, David invited me to dinner next time I was acting in New York or New Jersey. He promised there wouldn't be any strings attached, nor would there be any sex because I was a very nice lady. He genuinely liked me, he stated.

Although David seemed to be an extremely nice guy, I could not fulfill his dinner desires, much to his great disappointment. However, we did get to talk again a few times. Each time, he would always take over the sexy talk after I started it. I got used to his style, and we got along very well.

* * * *

Jody's Sleeping Aid

Tom called in the middle of the night, from Chicago, complaining he had insomnia. He thought I would be more fun than a sleeping pill, he said. Then, he told me he wanted to get his mind off work and that was tough to do because he worked on The Board of Trade.

He continued telling me he had come home alone from a party and had gone to bed, and found himself tossing and turning before he gave up, got up, and dialed for me. Now he wanted a different kind of party, one-on-one. Since it was below freezing in Chicago that night, he wanted our private fantasy-party in front of his wood-burning fireplace.

Then, Tom proceeded to tell me he was an ass man. He loved to touch women's asses, to feel them, to massage them, to look at them, and he especially loved to have anal sex, although he made a point of saying he loved other kinds of sex, too. Tom went on to tell me he collected layout shots of women exposing their derrieres. He felt he was an expert on the subject of women's asses.

Tom's fantasy starts with him serving me champagne while we are lounging on a large sofa in front of his fireplace. He unbuttons my silk blouse and removes it. He unzips my skirt and pulls it off me. Then, Tom finishes undressing me. He lies back on the couch and puts me on top of him. I sit straight up on him and grind my ass into his groin as we fuck in this position. Then, Tom gently pushes me off him and asks me to suck him, which I immediately do. As he is close to cumming, Tom has me stop and lie on the sofa with my butt somewhat raised. He goes behind me, and slowly, carefully, has anal sex with me. He progressively picks up the pace of the anal sex until he has a huge orgasm.

I could tell right away that Tom was feeling a whole lot mellower after he came. He said he was ready to go back to bed, and sleep like a rock. It was clear he wasn't going to need sleeping pills that night, for sure!

Continued from page 285

Erotic film stars, female and male, decide for themselves whether or not they will do such scenes, if asked to do one by a filmmaker. Producers and directors have always been able to get others to do that particular kind of scene, if their stars determine it's not for them. However, the majority of stars usually say yes.

Due to the nature of these scenes, though, both the female and male stars are particular with whom they will work. It's very important that the people involved in doing anal sex scenes have a sense of trust and respect for their film partners.

The scenes are carefully shot on closed sets with only a skeleton crew present, as are most sex scenes in movies.

Lots of callers would ask questions about filming erotic scenes, including these kinds, regardless what their own personal fantasies included. A good number of the callers who primarily had anal sex fantasies also had other sexual desires they wanted as foreplay, in their fantasies, preceding their ultimate turn on. Only a very few wished for anal sex phone fantasies exclusively.

In the process of doing calls, I learned very quickly

their erotic interests, including anal sex. The callers, who were especially interested in these kinds of fantasies, came from all kinds of backgrounds and education. Some were very well-educated sophisticates, and others were just the opposite. The anal-sex fantasies were not influenced by the ages of the callers, as well. Young men and older men were just as likely to have these fantasies, as they were to have some other fantasies.

Continued on page 298

A Real Ass Man

One cool spring evening, I received a call from Jeff, who resided in New Haven, Connecticut. Jeff had been lying on his oversized, plush white couch, watching the flames in his stone fireplace, and fantasizing I was with him. After awhile, Jeff decided to call me so he could get the most fulfillment from his fantasizing.

Although Jeff, a small business owner, had been

trying to have calls with me for months, this was the first time I had ever talked to him. He described himself as having chestnut brown hair, and deep blue eyes. He said he stood 6 feet 2 inches tall and weighed 195 pounds. Jeff continued to say he was about forty years old and had a nearly 10-inch cock, which was about two inches wide, (his description), when really turned on. There was something else Jeff wanted me to know. He said he was a "real ass man." A woman's ass was always in first place with him and nice breasts came in second. At this point, Jeff was ready for his sexual phone fantasies to be fulfilled.

The phone fantasy begins with Jeff lying back on the couch, and I am between his legs sucking his cock. He wants it with lots of verbalized action. Then, Jeff reaches for me and I turn around, so that we "69." Jeff is breathing hard as he tells me he wishes to rim me. His phone fantasy continues as he hotly licks me where he wishes to put his cock. Now, Jeff requests I turn around and get on my knees and elbows as he gets behind me and plays with my ass, rubbing his hard cock against it. Finally, Jeff tells me he wants to fuck me in the ass, which he instantly does. He is groaning loud and long as we talk about his long, hard, deep strokes. Suddenly, he lets out a yell as he cums anally.

After his orgasm, Jeff was ready to sleep. He talked about how wonderful he felt and how glad he was to finally talk to me. Jeff said he was so relaxed he could spend the night right there on the couch, the place of his fantasy. As he said good night, Jeff told me to expect more calls from him.

* * * *

Back Door Fantasy

I received a call, one evening, from Mario, a small animal veterinarian, in Ontario, Canada. Initially, Mario talked about his career as a vet, and how much he enjoyed it. Then, he told me he had seen several of my movies and that he was impressed by me, which lead to questions, such as how I got into erotic films, and who was my favorite male co-star.

After several of these questions, Mario is ready for his phone sex fantasy. He has me lying on a king-sized bed with a brass headboard. Mario walks into the bedroom and sees me looking seductive in a sheer blue teddy. He comes over to the side of the bed and I begin undressing him. I encourage Mario to lie on the bed, so that I can suck him.

While I am sucking him, he suddenly interrupts

me to ask more questions. This time, he wants to know if there is someone special in my life, and what are my feelings on anal sex.

Following these questions, Mario requests that I continue sucking him.

Then, he interrupts me, again, to tell me he wants to have anal sex with me. He unsnaps the crotch of my teddy and pushes it up to my waist. He asks that I lie on my stomach and raise my ass really high. We have anal sex and he climaxes.

It seemed Mario had planned part of his fantasy before he called, which was not unusual for a caller to do. However, it was somewhat unusual for a caller to interrupt in the middle of the fantasy sex to ask unrelated questions. I assumed, perhaps, he was too ready, too soon, and wanted to slow himself down. If that was the case, it seemed to work and he was able to control himself until what he considered the right time.

* * * *

No Dirty Talk

Jay called from Philadelphia, on a crisp January mid-evening. He immediately described himself as short, with light brown hair, baby blue eyes, and a 42-inch chest. He said he would be twenty-seven years old in two months, and he lifted weights as a hobby. He used to be a runner as well, but gave up running because of his career. Jay was a surgeon.

Then, Jay told me about his various favorites. His number one turn ons were sexy lingerie, seductive smiles, women's pretty pussies, and romantic talk. He loved oral sex and anal sex, too. Jay's top fantasies included having two girls at the same time and having sex with me (even if it were only fantasy sex).

After that, Jay suddenly sounded more somber. He told me he was broken-hearted. His long-time girlfriend had recently broken up with him. They had gone together for several years, and he had assumed they would be getting married in the future. However, about two weeks previous, she had dropped the bomb. They were through because she had met another man. To make it worse, in Jay's eyes, she was already planning on marrying the new man in her life.

Jay continued talking about his ex-girlfriend, Cathy, and how he always treated her romantically, and that he was a caring lover. He said she was beautiful with emerald green eyes, and long mahogany brown hair. He couldn't figure out how to move on, after losing her, so he called me.

We were about to enter Jay's fantasy world, but he told me one more thing before we did. Jay did not like dirty talk. He wanted us to only use "nice" words during the fantasy part of his call.

Jay's fantasy phone sex begins with us in chalet in the mountains in front of an oversized stone fireplace, drinking red wine. We are naked and I am teasing him with little touches and rubs of various parts of his body. He responds in a positive manner, and kisses me on my lips, my breasts, and continues with his kisses down to his favorite area. He spreads my legs apart and begins kissing and licking me, and practicing cunnilingus on me. Then, he turns around and has me practice fellatio on him, at the same time, (a.k.a. 69ing). Finally, Jay wants to have anal sex with me. He has me lying on my side with my derriere arched toward him. He takes me from behind. This is the position we are in, in the phone fantasy, when he orgasms.

After the phone sex, Jay told me I was totally different from anyone else with whom he had ever had a conversation. He said he genuinely liked me. Jay added he felt a little better too, about the ex-girlfriend, at least for that one night. I knew Jay was going to hurt for a time, but I knew he would heal by his last question before we hung up. He asked me if he could have the two-girl fantasy next time we talked.

Continued from page 292

The only thing I learned that the majority of the anal fantasy callers generally had in common, but not all by any means, was that they thought of themselves as "ass men." They particularly loved to look at, and admire, women's derrieres; just as some other men especially love to look at women's breasts.

The callers with anal-sex fantasies always seemed to enjoy our entertaining conversations. They never held back their most hidden desires from me, and, after the first few months with Personal Services, I was rarely surprised what their secret fantasies really were.

AFTER THOUGHTS

I have given the reader a taste of fantasy phone sex, by writing about just a few of my calls that I had during a year-and-a-half period of the twelve years I was with Personal Services Club. Deciding which calls to write about this first time was not always easy, as there were so many I wanted to share. I did not use any scientific means of picking and choosing for this book. I simply wrote about some of my favorites and some of my not-so-favorites, so that the reader got a generally accurate feel for the types of calls, and what the callers were like.

Some of my callers came across the phone lines as sexy studs; others seemed like lost, lonely souls, wanting to communicate with a female, who represented the ultimate hot woman in their eyes – an erotic film star. There were businessmen, too busy to enjoy a special intimacy with a woman, so grabbed what they could, in 15-minute intervals. Unhappy husbands, who would never dream of stepping out on their wives, felt safe and satisfied making calls. Other callers had physical disabilities, which they felt prevented them from having women as they wanted them. For the time period we were on the phone, their disabilities disappeared.

Strange and unusual fantasy calls could be exposed to me, although never known in those particular callers' real worlds. Some people wanted to fantasize about threesomes and orgies, only would never really do that except in their calls. Same-sex fantasies could be shared with me, but not with the people with whom those particular callers associated.

There were others, of course, the fetishists, the young, shy adult males, the horny drunks, the lovers, and my very special fans. Oh, yes, there were the callers who never wanted fantasy phone sex, but wished only to chat or to "interview" me.

During this same year and a half of having calls, I also had a very small number of calls so bizarre and over-the-edge that I decided not to put them in this book. They were anomalies, so were definitely not representative of any typical, or even untypical, phone sex call. However, I may decide to include some of them in future writings.

I, again, became a student of the human mind over the years I had fantasy phone sex calls. I relearned, from my callers the uniqueness and individuality of the human psyche. Yes, many callers had similar desires, i.e., oral sex, but their desires would somehow be different from others wishing for the same thing. I never allowed myself to forget each of these callers was an individual with special, unique fantasies, or the fact that the brain was the most powerful sex organ of all!

Some calls were dream calls to do; occasionally others were so tough and hard to do, that I felt a masochist might have been more suitable completing those calls. Fortunately, I only rarely felt that way about a call.

My callers occasionally sent me their pictures; sometimes, dressed and sometimes naked. Some would send me fan mail. Others purchased fan club items. Then, there were those who sent me gifts, like the pretty black Bali bra I found in my mail one day.

I developed my own clientele, the callers who would faithfully call me time and time again, over the years. I got to know some of them, through calls, pretty well. I knew everything about them from the names of their cocker spaniels to their ex-wives' measurements. I discovered in many cases I became their sounding boards to whom they could bare their souls. Those callers always felt better by the time we finished the calls.

Overall, I had a fascinating and fun time doing fantasy phone sex calls. Sometimes, my experiences were just plain funny, too. Many calls constantly reminded me that eroticism and humor often are considered strange bedfellows, but are bedfellows just the same.

I enjoyed sharing some of my calls by writing this book. However, the stories in **My Private Calls** were only the appetizer. Those readers with larger appetites should watch for Book 2, with the true stories of more of my calls to "cum."

ABOUT JODY MAXWELL

Jody Maxwell, a Kansas City, Missouri native, and the daughter and granddaughter, of prominent trial attorneys, won a 4-year scholarship to her private all-girls' high school. While there, Jody nurtured her writing skills, finally becoming the Managing Editor of her school newspaper and being published as one of the Outstanding High School Writers in America.

Jody is a graduate of the University of Missouri, where she majored in theatre and speech, and furthered her acting in legitimate theatre and in summer stock.

She began her career in erotica, after being discovered at a morality symposium on campus, shortly before graduation from the University, by Gerard Damiano, who was a member of the symposium.

After graduation, she starred in her first erotic, full-feature film, **Portrait**, written and directed by Damiano. Critics, and industry icons, such as Al Goldstein and Larry Flynt, immediately considered her the crowning successor to Linda Lovelace's title, with her versatile and unique talents and abilities.

Following the release of **Portrait** her career in erotica by adding a sexy, stand-up, comedic stage show, which she performed throughout the country; and by writing for men's magazines.

Previously, Jody was on the staff of several national men's magazines, including **Cheri**, **Escapade**, **Capers**, **Partner**, and **Adult Cinema Review.** had her own monthly column in a few of these magazines. She also wrote feature stories for them.

Eventually, Jody joined Personal Services Club, and had erotic, fantasy phone calls with members, for twelve years, during which she kept detailed notes in journals of each and every one of the thousands of calls she received.

Jody has starred in some of the greatest erotic movies of all time, including such classic hits as **Outlaw Ladies**; **Neon Nights**; **Satisfiers of Alpha Blue**; **Expose Me, Lovely**; **S.O.S.**; and **Devil Inside Her,** among others.

True to Jody's eclectic nature, she has had a full and rich history in politics, as well. She held many offices in the Young Republicans and attended Young Republican National Leadership Training School, in Washington, D.C. She has known many famous, political figures and officeholders, and previously has been a guest at the White House.

of education. Currently, she is writing a novel, and is also working on Book 2 of **My Private Calls**, in which she shares more of her intimate and intriguing phone calls.

Some of Jody's favorites are books, bowling, cooking, football, baseball, animals, and computers.

She resides in California.

To find out more about Jody, please visit her website at www.jodymaxwell.com.

* * * *

Dear Readers:

I am collecting other people's phone sex fantasies and experiences, for a future book. If you would be interested in contributing to my book, please send me the details of the call and fantasy, and as much as possible about yourself and the person to whom you were speaking. You may send me your information by any of the following ways: my website, email address, or through the mailing address listed below.

www.jodymaxwell.com

fantasies@jodymaxwell.com

Jody Maxwell
P.O. Box 26185
Overland Park, Kansas 66225-6185

Meanwhile, be sure and watch for the second book of **My Private Calls**.

* * * *

The audio version of My Private Calls, read by the premier mouth maven, Jody Maxwell, will soon be available exclusively on her website, www.jodymaxwell.com.

CPSIA information can be obtained
at www.ICGtesting.com
Printed in the USA
BVHW031416171122
652201BV00008B/262